A House

Is a Broken Home

Patron Gold

ISBN 978-0-615-51574-8

Printed in the United States of America
Editing/Typesetting: U Can Mark My Word
Cover Design: *www.tspubcreative.com*

Dedications

In loving memory of:

Elder Anthony Moses
Frances Sarah Moses
Betty Ann Moses
Tony Moses
Jamar Moses
Carl Moses
Elaine Moses

Acknowledgements

Allah: I thank you for the gift of literature. I thank you for blessing me to commit to this project.

To my family: Thank you for supporting me throughout this journey, I love you all!

U Can Mark My Word: Thank you so much for doing the interior design for me!

www.tspubcreative.com: Thank you for the great cover!

To my colleagues and friends: I thank you all for your advice. Also, thank you for lending an ear when I needed one.

Patron

A House
Is a Broken Home

By

Patron Gold

Introduction

It was the summer of 1980 in Brooklyn, New York. The sun rose in the early morning of the humid city as the sound of chirping birds echoed throughout the still air. Just hours ago, the neighborhood had been filled with life and activity. Friday nights were celebrated like a national holiday, but the streets were now deserted. As daybreak set in, everybody scattered like cockroaches do when the lights are turned on in the middle of the night.

The neighborhood was comprised of a Black and Hispanic community, with a bodega erected on almost every street corner. The bodegas were convenient, especially for the parents who sent their kids on errands because they were too lazy to walk up the street themselves. There was no age restriction. A six-year-old could buy beer or cigarettes as long as they had a handwritten note from an adult, but returning home empty handed was not an option. If the bodega on your street corner didn't have what you wanted, then you had to find one that did.

In the center of this nostalgic era, an old tenement building that sheltered twelve families stood parallel to the ruins of a vacant lot, which had long ago been rejected by the city officials. The neighborhood kids, however, used the vacancy of the lot to their advantage. With the use of their imaginations, they took huge quantities of the debris and built defense barriers to play War, while a disregarded bed mattress served its purpose as a boxing ring for Fight Night.

Upstairs in apartment 4-C, Keisha struggled to get out of bed. She had hosted a card party with her boyfriend Sonny last night, and it lasted until the wee hours of the morning. A typical card party included music, food, and plenty of alcohol. It was a form of socializing without having to spend a lot of money, but it was also an alternative to keep Sonny from hanging out in the streets at night.

After she freshened up and threw on a bathrobe, Keisha walked into the kitchen to prepare breakfast. She got three spoons from the silverware drawer and opened the cabinets for the cereal bowls. Upon looking inside, she discovered there were only two bowls remaining from a recently purchased set.

"That damn Cece's got all of my dishes. She never returns anything," she uttered.

Keisha searched high and low for something that could substitute for a third bowl. She finally came across an aluminum pie pan that contained some leftover food in the fridge. Keisha rinsed the pan in the sink and then sat at the breakfast table. Having consumed far too many drinks last night, the aftermath started to kick in. Keisha removed a pack of cigarettes from her robe and lit one. The first drag made her lightheaded, as usual. Now in a hypnotic state of mind, Keisha began to retrace accounts from her past.

Keisha Johnson had always been an ambitious young lady. Her goal was to become a registered nurse after graduation. During high school, she maintained a grade point average that excelled above others in her class, and she graduated with honors. Unfortunately, her parents could not afford to pay for her college tuition. Determined to pursue her dream, Keisha enrolled at a community college and worked part-time to support herself. However, a sequence of events took place that would forever change the course of her life.

Chapter 1
Rewind

One night during the fall of '75, Keisha and her best friend, Cece Harris, visited The Mixer, a local nightclub. It was there Keisha met her first love interest, Alvin "Detroit" Williams. Detroit was a musician who performed at the club on weekends. It was a known fact that Detroit was a ladies' man, and it was very rare to find him without a woman on his arm. Detroit was also a flashy dresser. He never shopped at department stores; all of his suits were tailor made.

Percy Solomon ran the nightclub. He was in his early forties and of average size, but well respected in the community. In addition to the nightclub, Percy owned a numbers hole that fronted as a candy store. He conducted the business from behind a bulletproof glass window.

The Mixer had a pleasant aura; it provided live entertainment and even served breakfast before closing. Overall, the atmosphere was quite enjoyable.

The girls lucked out on getting a ride to the club like they normally did, so they rode the city bus instead. It was far from riding in luxury, but it got them to their destination. Cece brought an umbrella, which they shared. It was a short distance from the bus stop to the streetlight at the corner, but it was freezing outside and felt like it had taken them forever to reach it. Furthermore, the cheap umbrella did not withstand the force of the wind; it blew behind them as they walked. Fortunately, the nightclub was just across the street.

When the traffic cleared, Keisha and Cece made a run for it. The sharpness of the wind and freezing rain blurred their vision as it hit their faces. They stopped under the awning above the club's doorway. Their overcoats were completely drenched. They couldn't walk inside the nightclub the way they were, so they took turns brushing each other off. Once they were presentable, Keisha rang the doorbell.

Moe, the attendant, looked through the peephole. He was a regular at the barbershop that Keisha's dad owned on Sutter Avenue. His large frame towered over them as the door opened.

"Shit, it's colder than a witch's titty outside! Y'all come on in here where it's warm," he said while taking their coats.

"Ain't it, though?" Cece replied. "We really do appreciate you waiting on us, Moe!"

"Yeah, thanks a lot, Moe," Keisha said and kissed him on the cheek.

Moe cracked a smile, showing partial teeth and bare gums. Back in his heyday, Moe was an amateur boxer, but not a very good one. He experienced more than his share of ass whippings in the ring than he cared to admit. However, he still handled himself pretty well, which was one of the reasons Percy kept him around.

It was only 11:00 p.m., but the club was packed. After finding the restroom, Keisha and Cece fixed their hair and makeup. When they came out, Cece spotted a table.

"There's one," she pointed out. "Let's hurry up and get it before someone else does."

Keisha nodded in agreement and followed Cece through the crowd. Just as they were within reach of the table, a tall, skinny, country brother bumped into Cece and stepped on her foot.

"Ouch! Are you fucking blind?" she screamed.

The startled man turned around and eyeballed Cece from head

13

to toe. Cece had a pretty ebony complexion, brown eyes, and was stacked. She was wearing a one-piece mini outfit that exposed her midriff and clung tightly to her visually plump derriere.

Damn, she swoller than a fat swamp possum wit' a rutabaga in its mouth, he thought. "My bad," he explained. "I'm Leroy. Let me buy you a drank."

"A drank," Cece said, mimicking him. "Man, if you don't get your country ass out my face..." Cece drew her hand upward and reached into her bra.

Keisha cringed. *Oh shit, she's going for the switchblade!*

Cece was not the one to mess with; she knew how to strap. Keisha had witnessed Cece beat the living crap out of grown men who thought she was defenseless, but found out otherwise. Keisha grabbed hold of Cece's arm and tried to calm her down.

"Come on, Cece. Let's go," she pleaded.

Cece had drawn attention. One of the bouncers spotted the incident and came over to investigate.

"Is there a problem, ladies?" he asked.

Cece stood with her hands on her hips. She was hot and ready to jump on Leroy at any moment.

"There sure is," Cece exclaimed. "This fool right here."

Keisha cut in, "No, no problem at all."

Cece looked at Keisha like she had just been betrayed.

"Well then, y'all need to clear this area," the bouncer said and walked away.

"Come on, girl," Keisha said, nudging Cece along.

"Yeah, you're right, girl. Let's go before somebody in here gets hurt!" Cece agreed.

She bucked at Leroy, making him flinch before they walked away. Keisha confronted Cece when they were seated at the table.

"Girl, you are something else. We haven't been in here ten minutes, and you already showing out!"

Cece placed her leg up on the table and removed her shoe,

baring a big knot along her outer toe.

"Look at this shit, Keisha," she said. "But I'm showing out, right?"

Keisha glanced at Cece's foot and shook her head. "Girl, that's a damn bunion. Your shoes are too tight," she said.

They both laughed and gave each other dap to assure there was no tension.

Keisha and Cece were like sisters. They grew up on the same block and had known each other since kindergarten. During her junior year, Cece dropped out of high school and gave birth to her son Jahlil by her seventeenth birthday. Around that time, Keisha slept over Cece's house on weekends. Cece's mom, Clara, believed Keisha set a good example for her daughter to follow. Had she known the girls paid someone to watch Jahlil and went partying while she was at work, it would have been another story.

The girls basked in the limelight. They had hung out in little hole-in-the-wall bars around the neighborhood, but The Mixer was a new venue. Since its beginning, The Mixer had always been the center of attraction, exclusively to people of color. Of course, there were other places in the city for entertainment, but The Mixer was in the heart of the ghetto. It was a temple of solace for poverty stricken blacks who had nothing else to look forward to besides having a good time when they could afford it. For some, it was a weekend haven.

Keisha searched through her purse for cigarettes. From the humbled look on Cece's face, she could tell she wanted one, too. Cece smoked twice the amount Keisha did, but never supplied her own pack. Keisha offered her a smoke, and they lit up.

Percy Solomon emerged from his office and looked around at his establishment in satisfaction. It was a full house, which meant a prosperous intake for the night. He reached into the breast pocket of his blue sharkskin suit blazer and withdrew an imported Cuban cigar, which he lit. Then, he lifted a fine gold antique pocket watch from his crisp pleated trousers. It was time to announce the band. With a snap of his fingers, Percy had the deejay's attention. The music stopped, and the houselights dimmed. Percy stood in the spotlight at center stage and grabbed the microphone.

"First off, I'd like to thank you all for coming out tonight," he said.

Thunderous applause and loud shouting from the partygoers interrupted Percy's speech. Once the crowd settled down, he continued.

"Wait a minute. Let me finish. Before you all got happy, I was also going to say that in appreciation of your ongoing support, the next round of drinks is on me!"

He soon found out that the mention of free alcohol was a big mistake. Like a herd of wild animals, people surrounded the bar within seconds, and Percy had to restore order. Again, he took the microphone.

"Hit the lights and close the bar!" he yelled.

The emphasis of anger in Percy's voice silenced the room. The houselights came on, exposing the uncivilized acts happening at the bar. His eyes pierced the room with a look of disgust.

Percy was a self-made man who took pride in his nightclub. However, he had obtained it at a costly price. Percy was a criminal, so he stayed in court battling the city health inspectors from closing him down. He also operated an illegal gambling racket, which the cops leaned on him for kickbacks. Percy paid the bribery, and the cops looked the other way.

Upon finally noticing the displeased look on Perry's face as he stared at them, the majority of the house settled down, but a count of five heads remained at the bar, hoping to score a free drink. The rest of the crowd awaited Percy's next move. Percy directed his attention to the bar, where the bouncers were already positioned.

"See, this is the kinda shit that happens when you try to be nice! You give a nigga an inch, and he takes the whole yard! I want every last one of you thirsty bastards to get the hell out of my nightclub, and I mean right fucking now!"

The bouncers escorted the humiliated group to the door.

"Y'all get the fuck on, and don't bother coming back!" Moe said as he led them out.

Once again, Percy addressed the audience.

"Okay, let's get this show started," he said. "Without further ado, ladies and gentlemen, please put your hands together for Entourage!"

The five-member ensemble entered the stage. The up-tempo song kicked off with an intense series of drum rolls, followed by a soulful chorus of riffs by the lead singer. The nightclub erupted into an explosive uproar. The women, who responded to the local band as if they were rock stars, broke through the barrier of security like groupies and swarmed the stage area screaming hysterically. Some of the women removed their panties, big and small, tossing them onto the stage. Before long, the destabilized women were uncontrollable and had to be restrained

Chapter 2
Chance Meeting

Despite the chaos, Keisha and Cece managed to get close enough to the stage to enjoy the performance. Keisha found a few of the band members attractive, but it was Detroit who caught her eye. He was dapper and strikingly handsome, but he was also more experienced than any of the guys she had dated in the past. Keisha was also aware of Detroit's reputed history with womanizing, but she was willing to risk the chance if opportunity ever presented itself.

Detroit had taken an interest in Keisha, as well. While performing, he noticed an exceptionally attractive young woman checking him out. His first impression was that she was just another groupie. But, after more observation, he realized he had judged wrong. She wasn't loud and obnoxious like the rest of the women, and she didn't make a spectacle of herself. She was a lady. Of course, he could have chosen any of the women who were in the club; that was without question. However, it had been a while since he earned a woman's confidence, and he was eager to accept the challenge. Besides, they had already made a connection. After the set, he would formally introduce himself.

The band performed a string of hits that were current on the airwaves, and they ended the show with a classic track. The gathering of spectators caused the nightclub to draw heat. Dehydrated, Keisha proposed to Cece that they go over to the bar for refreshments. Moreover, she wanted to talk to her. Keisha was strongly considering the possibility of striking up a conversation with Detroit, but she was undecided.

Will he be interested? she wondered.

The girls entered the bar area and sat in two empty seats at the far end. They tried to wave Otis, the bartender, over to them, but he was busy serving customers. Otis was old and slower than molasses; still, everyone liked him. Finally, they succeeded in catching his attention. Keisha ordered two rum and cokes. Then she started talking with Cece while they waited on the drinks.

"Cece, what would you say if I told you that I was thinking of getting up with Detroit? I think he's cute. Don't you?"

Cece looked at Keisha like she was crazy. "Aw, hell no!" she replied. "Keisha, have you lost your damn mind? First of all, he looks damn near ten years older than you. He probably wouldn't give you the time of day, let alone hook up with you. And secondly, you know about that man's reputation. He's probably messing around with more women than you can count on both hands. So, leave it alone!"

Keisha responded, "Age ain't nothing but a number. The two people involved in the relationship are all that matters. Besides, what makes you think he wouldn't be interested? He noticed me, I think."

"Yeah, he noticed you were easy," Cece told her. "But, don't take my word for it. Go right ahead; you'll see."

Otis returned with the drinks. "Here you are, ladies. That'll be ten dollars," he said.

As Keisha reached into her purse to pay the tab, Detroit walked up from behind and stood between her and Cece. He pulled out his wallet and handed Otis a twenty.

"Here you go, Otis. And while you're at it, I'll have a scotch on the rocks, if you don't mind."

Otis pushed Detroit's hand away. "Now you know your

money's no good around here. Don't insult me like that," he replied.

Detroit put the folded bill into Otis's tip jar and gave him a wink. "Well, my brotha, you can't say I didn't try."

A big grin emerged on Otis's face, "My man! That's what I'm talking about!" Otis took the money from the tip jar and put it right in his pocket.

Keisha turned to face Detroit and thank him, but she was taken by his appearance. *This is one well-groomed man,* she thought. His hair was styled in a 360-degree spinning wave pattern, which blended perfectly with his smooth caramel skin tone. He was also well dressed, and the scent of his cologne was alluring.

Detroit was also enticed by Keisha. Her creamy fair skin was flawless, and her smile was irresistible. His eyes traced along the contours of Keisha's well-rounded bottom and watched it protrude through the form-fitting skirt she was wearing. Finally, he addressed them.

"Allow me to introduce myself, ladies. I'm Alvin Williams, but my friends call me Detroit," he said, extending his hand.

Cece looked at Detroit's hand like it was infectious. "Well, I ain't your friend," she said, then downed the drink and walked off.

"You'll have to excuse my friend. She acts out at times," explained Keisha. "By the way, I'm Keisha. Thanks for the drinks."

"You're quite welcome," Detroit replied. "So, tell me, Keisha, how old are you?"

"I'm eighteen, and I live with my parents. But, I also have a job and am studying to be a nurse," she clarified. "What about yourself?"

"Well, I'm twenty-four years old, and when I'm not performing, I work as an accountant for an office firm," Detroit replied.

After exchanging likenesses, Keisha and Detroit saw that they were compatible. They chatted a while longer, and before they knew it, it was nearly two o'clock in the morning. Detroit threw a coin in the jukebox and selected a slow track. When he asked Keisha to dance with him, she obliged without hesitation.

Detroit took Keisha by the hand and led her to the dance floor. The club was nearly empty now as people gathered their belongings and started to leave. Cece sat alone at one of the tables, impatiently checking the time on the big clock that hung on the wall. She had met someone earlier, but he was long gone. Just as luck would have it, he didn't own a car and left to catch the last bus. As much as Cece hated the idea, she would have to wait on Keisha and catch a ride with Detroit. Besides, they came to the club together, and they were going to leave together, she decided.

Back on the floor, Detroit rested his hands on the small of Keisha's back, while she put her arms around his broad shoulders. He pulled her closely and felt the firmness of her breasts as they pressed against him. When their eyes locked, Detroit leaned forward and planted a long, passionate kiss onto Keisha's receiving lips.

When the song ended, the house lights came on. Cece had watched Keisha and Detroit for the entirety of the dance. Keisha's behavior sickened her. *What can she possibly see in that two-timing snake?* she thought.

"I'm about to put an end to this bullshit right now," she uttered. "Um, excuse me, Keisha!" she shouted. "Some of us have to go to work in the morning. You need to handle your business so we can go!"

Keisha turned to Cece with a look of scorn. *This bitch got some nerve. Like I never waited on her ass before,* she thought.

Detroit couldn't help but laugh. He thought Cece was comical.

"I guess your girl is ready to go," he said humorously. "Where do you live?"

"Over on Herzl Street," Keisha answered. "Cece isn't getting on your nerves yet, is she?"

"Nah, she's cool," Detroit assured her. "Let me bring the car around, and I'll meet you up front."

Keisha and Cece got their coats from Moe and waited with him inside the doorway. Detroit pulled up in his mint-green Cadillac convertible and honked the horn.

"Y'all get home safe now, ya hear?" Moe said as he opened the door to let them out.

Keisha rode up front with Detroit, while Cece sat directly behind her in the backseat. During the drive, Keisha and Detroit recapped the night and exchanged phone numbers. When they reached Keisha's block, she instructed Detroit to let them out a few doors down from Cece's house. It had stopped raining. Without thanking Detroit for the ride, Cece jumped out of the car and slammed the door behind her as she went to her neighbor's house to get Jahlil.

While opening the car door, Keisha turned to Detroit and said, "Well, this is my stop. Thanks again for the ride. I had a wonderful time tonight."

"Same here. I had a good time," Detroit replied. He leaned over to kiss Keisha goodnight, but she pushed him away.

"Not here," she said. "I have to go now, but call me."

"Sure thing, baby. I'll do just that."

Detroit watched as she ran up the driveway. After she disappeared behind the front door, he drove off.

Chapter 3
Get In Where You Fit In

Throughout the next week, Keisha went about her normal routine. She went to school during the morning hours and met up with Cece in the afternoon to work the cash register at the neighborhood supermarket. She constantly reminded herself of the scenario at the nightclub. Keisha was tempted to call Detroit, but she didn't want to seem desperate. If anyone were to call first, it would be him.

Meanwhile, Detroit resumed his position at the numbers hole on Saratoga Avenue. As he went over the books, he thought about Keisha and remembered telling her that he was an accountant. Technically, his occupation was against the law, but he had told her the truth. All of Detroit's obligations to Percy were strictly clerical; in other words, he helped control the books. Keisha was too young to be exposed to this kind of lifestyle. *The less she knows, the better,* he thought. Yet, his impulse to see her urged him to reconsider his own advice.

Later that evening, Detroit closed the store down and returned to the upper east side of Manhattan. As he entered his one-bedroom apartment on Park Avenue and 5th, he kicked out of his shoes and hung his designer cashmere overcoat in the hall closet. Detroit's pad was stylish and immaculately kempt. In fact, it was one of the more extravagant homes in the entire unit. However, the white residents who lived in the building were not at all receptive to their black neighbor. Detroit wasn't offensive; they just refused to give him a chance. Instead, they dubbed him as a bougie nigger with money, and avoided him at all cost. Whenever he passed them in the halls or on the street, they stuck their noses in the air and pretended not to see him.

The property owner was a middle-aged man named Francesco, who hailed from Italy. He and Detroit got along just fine. When Detroit first inquired about moving into the building, Francesco asked Detroit what he did for a living. Detroit introduced himself as a musician and told Francesco that he played in a band at a nightclub. The wheels quickly turned in Francesco's head. He saw this as an opportunity to meet young black tail, which he was fond of. Detroit guaranteed that he would deliver on time, and Francesco leased the apartment to him, as per their agreement. In order to keep his end of the bargain, Detroit hired a prostitute every so often and sent her over to see Francesco. Francesco was none the wiser, but he was content.

Chapter 4
Meet the Johnsons

Detroit poured himself a scotch on the rocks, just as he did each time he came in from a hard day's work, and sat on the sofa. He picked up the evening paper from the coffee table and fumbled through it until he found the sports section. It wasn't long before he became bored with the article and threw the paper down on the coffee table.

He thought about Keisha again. It had been a week since they first met. He had to call her, and now was as good a time as any. He recalled Keisha saying she got off work at six o'clock, and it was now a little past seven p.m. Detroit considered that Keisha still lived with her parents. He had just met her, so there was no need to jump to conclusions and get them involved yet. Detroit went into his wallet and got the paper napkin he had written Keisha's number on. As he proceeded to dial the seven digits, he prayed it would be Keisha who answered the phone. However, Keisha's mother, Victoria Johnson, picked up on the third ring. Despite their age difference, Keisha favored Victoria in every sense. In twenty years or so, she would be her mother's spitting image.

"Good evening, Johnson's residence. This is Victoria speaking," she said politely.

Detroit hesitated to speak. *Just my luck. It's her mother,* he thought before clearing his throat to speak.

"How are you, Mrs. Johnson? I'm Alvin Williams, a friend of

Keisha's. I hope I haven't called too late."

"I'm fine. Thank you for asking," Victoria responded. "And it isn't too late. I'll get Keisha for you." Victoria covered the receiver with her hand and yelled, "Keisha, come get the telephone!"

"I'll be right there, Mama!" Keisha yelled back from her bedroom. She soon approached Victoria from behind and tapped her on the shoulder. "Who is it, Mama?" she whispered.

"Girl, just take the phone. I'm not your messenger!" Victoria clarified.

Keisha put the phone to her ear. "Hello, this is Keisha."

"Hi, Keisha. This is Detroit. I hope I didn't disturb you."

Keisha's heart skipped a beat. She had waited all week for Detroit to call, and when he did, she panicked.

She took a deep breath and responded, "Not at all. I was in the bedroom listening to my new albums. So how are you, stranger?"

"I can't complain," he answered. "I'm just getting in myself. Figured I'd give you a call and see what you were up to. How are you?"

"I've been okay," Keisha answered. "I will admit that I'm surprised to hear from you. I thought you had forgotten about me."

"If I lived to be a hundred years old, I think I would remember you, Keisha."

"Oh, and why is that?" she asked.

"Well, for one thing, you do have a big future behind you."

"Flattery will get you nowhere, but I'll take that as a compliment," Keisha said.

"Anyway," Detroit continued, "what are your plans for this evening? I was thinking maybe we could get together and do something."

"I hadn't planned anything. What did you have in mind?"

"How about dinner?" Detroit asked. "I know a great little spot that serves the best Greek cuisine."

"That sounds interesting," Keisha remarked. "I've never tried it before, but what's there to lose, right?"

"Good! Then it's a date." Detroit then asked for her address, which he jotted down. "I'll see you in about an hour."

"That's fine. I'll meet you downstairs. See you soon."

Keisha placed the handset back on the base of the phone. After giving it some thought, she decided she'd share the good news with Cece. She dialed the number and waited as the phone rang continuously. Cece answered just as Keisha was about to hang up.

"Hello," Cece mumbled through a mouth full of Neapolitan ice cream.

"Well, it's about time!" Keisha said, now irritated. "Why did it take you so long to answer the phone? I was about to hang up on your ass!"

"Shut the hell up!" Cece snapped. "You wasn't gonna do shit but wait just like I taught you."

"I know damn well you ain't popping shit, Cece. I'll come over there right now and slap the shit out of you in front of your mama and that big-head baby."

Cece could not refrain from laughing herself. Jahlil's forehead was rather large for a toddler.

"I wish you would come over here, heifer. I bet you one thing; your mama won't recognize you when you get back! What you calling me for anyway?"

"Girl, you will never guess who just called me!"

"Ooh, was it that guy from earlier today? The one who honked at us?"

"You know damn well I'm not talking about him, Cece. Remember, we dipped into the store to get milk for bighead? We never talked to him."

"Keep on talking about my baby, and see if I don't bust your ass, Keisha."

"I'm just playing. You know I love my god-baby. Anyway, it was Detroit from the club. We're going out to dinner. Call one of your guy friends so we can double date."

"Thanks, but I'll have to pass on this one, girl. Nobody's trying to watch Jahlil tonight. I've already tried to find a babysitter. And you know my mama ain't gonna do it."

"Gee, that's too bad. I really wanted us to hang out," Keisha said. "Oh well, I'll call you in the morning. Sleep tight, bitch!"

"Same to you, hoe!" Cece replied.

Within the next hour, Detroit pulled up at Keisha's house and honked for her to come downstairs. After putting on her coat, Keisha grabbed her purse. Thomas, Keisha's father, stopped her at the door.

"Where in the world are you going this time of night?" he asked. "Every time I look around, you running the streets with that ol' fast girl, Cece. Most I ever see of you is the back of your head when you're leaving!"

"I'm not going out with Cece, Daddy. I have a dinner date."

"What, you too good to eat with us now? Your mama's got a great big ol' pot of neck bones on the stove. And who are you going out with?"

"He's a new friend, Daddy. Nobody you would know," Keisha answered.

"How could I know him? You never bring any of your boy friends around to meet me. Are you ashamed of me, girl?"

Keisha adored her father. Thomas was her knight in shining armor, and she was his little princess. At forty-five, Thomas had a beer belly and grey hair that sprouted throughout his fro, but he was still handsome.

Thomas had always provided well for his family, and he was a loving husband to his wife. However, there was one problem; he never wore any pants around the house. At the moment, he was wearing a wife beater that was tucked unevenly inside his striped flannel boxer shorts. Even worse, he scratched his head and passed gas as they talked.

"Ugh, Daddy! That was disgusting!" Keisha howled, covering her nose.

Victoria and T.J., Keisha's mother and older brother, came in from the family room. T.J. was stocky like his father. He was an avid bodybuilder and played football during high school. Like most fathers, Thomas hoped T.J. would achieve success through his athleticism, so he spent lots of hours training with him when he was younger. But, unlike Keisha, T.J. was lazy and had no self-motivation. At twenty-one, he still lived with his parents and had no intentions of moving out.

"What are you two in here fussing about now?" Victoria asked. "Y'all likely to wake the dead with all that noise!"

"And what is that smell?" T.J. added.

"Daddy just farted," Keisha said.

Victoria and T.J. covered their noses, as well.

"You see how she talks to me right, Vicky? That's your daughter," Thomas grumbled.

"Thomas Johnson, you leave her be. Keisha's not a child anymore. She's a young woman, and it's about time you start treating her like one."

Thomas threw his hands in the air. "I give up. Once again, I've been outnumbered. No thanks to you!" he said, pointing at T.J.

"Thanks, Ma. I love you both." Keisha kissed Thomas and Victoria, then rushed out the door.

Victoria returned to the family room, leaving Thomas and T.J. alone.

"T.J., why did you just stand there like a dummy? Don't you know how to open your mouth, boy?" Thomas asked.

"Pops, Mom's right. You don't have to worry about Keisha. She's a good girl," T.J. answered.

"Son, I think that was the dumbest thing you've ever said in your life. I'm not worried about Keisha, you damn fool; I'm worried about that boy she's with. I would ask you to follow her, but you'd probably get lost. Then I'd have to come out and find you, too!"

"Ha-ha. That was so funny I forgot to laugh, Pops."

"Keep it up, and you'll be laughing from the outside looking in!"

Chapter 5
Table for Two

Keisha was so anxious to get downstairs that she tripped and barely escaped a disastrous fall by holding onto the banister. Detroit peered over the steering wheel of his convertible with a sigh of relief when he saw her coming. He was slouched behind the wheel trying to hide. It was a risky move coming back to Keisha's neighborhood to begin with. The numbers hole was within walking distance from where she lived. He prayed none of the betting customers walked by and blew his cover. When Keisha got near, he reached over the passenger side to let her in.

"Hi," Keisha said as she climbed inside.

Detroit gave her a quick nod and looked at the gold Rolex on his arm. "It's about time," he said in a grumpy tone. "What took you so long? I saw you sitting in the window when I first rolled up, and that was like twenty minutes ago."

"I know, and I apologize," she said. "I ran into a little altercation with my father. He's forever treating me like a little girl."

"You'll always be your daddy's little girl no matter how old you get, so you might as well get used to it. Let's just forget about the whole thing. My stomach is talking, and that can only mean one thing. It's time to grub! Let's say we get out of here and grab something to eat."

"Sounds like a plan. I'm starving," Keisha replied.

*****

Detroit held the door open for Keisha as they entered Adelfo's, an authentic Greek restaurant in Greenwich Village. Adelfo flashed a welcoming smile from the kitchen as his wife Bernice greeted them. Bernice was a short, stout woman with heavily rouged cheeks and pudgy arms. After welcoming Detroit with a friendly hug, Bernice walked up to Keisha, who made a gesture to shake hands but quickly surrendered to Bernice's unexpected embrace. Keisha tried to understand why the strange woman, whom she had only met seconds ago, expressed such compassion towards her. Later, Detroit explained to her that it was a traditional custom practiced in the Greek culture. Finally, they were seated in a cozy booth along the wall. Bernice lit a candle set in a round goblet and placed it before them.

Keisha viewed the décor of the fancy dining facility. The tables were covered in white linen with gold trimming. There was a roaring fireplace, and the walls were covered with exotic scenes of the Mediterranean. *This is some classy joint*, she thought.

Bernice distributed menus to the couple, and then in her thick accent, she asked, "Can I bring you drinks now? If no, then take your time."

"No, I'm ready," Detroit said. "I'll have a cold beer. Thank you."

"And for you, miss?"

Keisha looked up. "I think I'll try a glass of the house wine, please."

"Very good choice. I will come back shortly," Bernice said.

Detroit looked at Keisha. Noticing she seemed a bit on edge, he offered her a cigarette and lit one for himself.

"Is there something wrong?" he asked. "You look uncomfortable."

"I'm fine," Keisha replied. "It's just that I've never been to a

33

place like this before. I feel like everyone is staring at me."

Detroit took Keisha's hand. Her fair skin glowed beyond the wavering candlelight. Keisha's hair was styled in a French bun, revealing almond-shaped cat-like eyes that hinted a trace of Asian descent in her heritage. She was stunning.

"If they are staring, it's only because you're so beautiful. I can't blame them for that."

"Thank you," Keisha replied. "You ain't too bad yourself."

Detroit laughed at the comment. "You're welcome," he said. "I would have told you earlier, but I was upset. I sat out there for a long time waiting on you."

"Is that why you were giving me the silent treatment the whole time during the ride here?"

"That's right. It was cold out there!"

"Just for that, I'm going to purposely be late the next time," Keisha joked.

"You better not, woman," Detroit shot back.

Bernice returned with the drinks. "Here we are. One cold beer for the gentleman and a nice wine for the young lady. Have we decided what to eat?" she asked.

Detroit ordered first. "I think I'll go with the grilled rib-eye steak and mushrooms."

Keisha picked the menu up and went down the list. Everything she saw was foreign to her, and she didn't like steak. She was so hungry that she would have settled for a two-piece snack with a biscuit. At last, she found a dish that she could identify.

"I'll have the gyro dinner and salad. Thank you."

"Very well," Bernice said, then took the menus and went to give the orders to Adelfo.

As Bernice walked away, a slim young man with dirty blonde hair walked up to the table carrying a violin. It was Giorgio, Adelfo and Bernice's youngest son. He placed the instrument under his chin and began to play. Keisha was fascinated by the serenade. It was unlike the music she was accustomed to hearing, but she appreciated the spontaneity of the occasion. When Giorgio was done, Keisha applauded, and Detroit tipped him generously.

Adelfo helped Bernice with the dinner cart. He was a robust man with thick, hairy forearms and a bushy mustache that curled up at the corners. Adelfo chatted with Detroit and Keisha briefly before he left them to enjoy their dinner. After the meal, they thanked everyone for the great service and left the restaurant.

Chapter 6
First Time's a Charm

Detroit talked Keisha into coming back to his place for a nightcap before he drove her back to Brooklyn, and she willingly accepted the offer. Keisha was having such a good time that she didn't want to end the date. The other reason she didn't want to go home was her father, Thomas. Keisha knew he would probably be sitting in the family room waiting on her, and she didn't feel like arguing with him tonight.

Give him a little more time, and he'll go to bed, she thought.

Keisha sat quietly on the sofa, while Detroit prepared drinks at the wet bar. Soon after, he joined her and set the serving tray on the coffee table. He removed a chilled bottle of champagne from the ice bucket, popped the cork, and poured evenly into two stemmed glasses. When the froth had settled, Detroit handed Keisha a drink and proposed a toast.

"To a wonderful evening," he said.

"To a wonderful evening," Keisha repeated.

They clinked glasses and drank from the champagne glasses with their arms intertwined and their eyes focused. Detroit kissed Keisha delicately on the lips, pulled back momentarily, and then reconnected. Keisha pulled him closer with her free hand, feeling the warmth of his breath.

Detroit eased Keisha's drink from her hand and carried her into the bedroom, where he carefully laid her on the bed and started nibbling behind her ear while unbuttoning her blouse. Keisha sighed as Detroit worked his hand into her bra and played with her erect nipples. He slid his hand under her skirt and eased his fingers into her now moistened panties. When Keisha felt the swell of his bulge against her leg, she sat up.

"Wait a minute. I have something to tell you," she said nervously, then lowered her head shamefully. "Detroit, I've never been with a man before. I'm a virgin," she confessed.

Confused, Detroit looked at Keisha. He could not believe what he had just heard. The possibility of her being a virgin had crossed his mind, but he let it go because her mentality was that of a grown woman. In any case, the surprising new revelation hastened his curiosity. Detroit ran his fingers through Keisha's hair and tried to comfort her.

"Look, baby," he began. "I'm really feeling you, but I won't force myself on you. I'll understand if you aren't ready for this."

Keisha wept and spoke softly. "I feel the same way about you, Dee. I have from the moment we met. I just don't want to get hurt."

Detroit wiped Keisha's tears away with the back of his hand.

"I would never hurt you, baby. I promise that on everything I love," he replied.

Keisha searched Detroit's eyes for the truth. She had always dreamed of losing her virginity to her husband on the night of their honeymoon. Nevertheless, Keisha had fallen hard for Detroit and desperately wanted him.

"I believe you, daddy," she said, then kissed him intensely.

Keisha bravely unhooked her bra and threw it across the chair in the corner of the room. She let the zipper down on the back of her skirt and let it fall to the floor. She then worked her way out of her underwear and pantyhose until they were down around her ankles. Standing before Detroit, Keisha straddled his leg. With her standing in front of him, he firmly grabbed her buttocks and played with them like putty in his hands.

Keisha unbuttoned Detroit's shirt and massaged his masculine torso, while he removed his slacks and then his silk boxers.

As she viewed Detroit's manhood for the first time, goose bumps elevated their way to the surface of Keisha's skin. The mere sight of it frightened her. It was huge, and it swung on its own accord. Keisha feared the monstrous instrument would tear her insides apart.

She pulled back from Detroit to catch her breath.

"Oh my God," she gasped, pointing at his erect muscle. "If you think you're putting that thing in me, think again!"

Detroit grinned. "Don't you go getting scared on me now, baby," he said. "Just sit back and relax. I'll take it from here."

Detroit kissed Keisha tenderly before laying her down on her back. Keisha's body quivered as his tongue darted along her neckline, cleverly maneuvering its way past her waistline. He slid his tongue to the hood of Keisha's aroused clitoris and then slowly parted her labium. He tasted her wet juices and teasingly bit on her inner thighs.

When Keisha was fully stimulated, Detroit climbed atop of her and gently inserted his tool. Keisha writhed frantically while biting her bottom lip as the force of Detroit's organ tore her hymen. Beads of sweat rolled off their bodies as the tension increased. The agonizing discomfort Keisha first experienced had been replaced with sexual desire. She secured her legs around Detroit's lower back and gyrated her hips at a riveted pace, timely meeting each of his thrusts as he worked her pelvic region in circular motions. At the height of Keisha's climax, she closed her eyes and dug her nails deep into Detroit's back as her body squirmed uncontrollably.

"Hold me, daddy. I'm cumming!" she squealed.

Keisha's plea invoked Detroit's ego even more. He gripped his arms tightly around her body and penetrated vigorously into her tunnel until his load erupted inside of her. Afterward, they lay in each other's arms and drifted into a slumber.

Chapter 7
Where am I?

The next morning, Keisha rolled onto her side and buried her face in the pillow to block the veil of sunlight shining through the window. As she shifted to a different position to get more comfortable, her senses became alert. The mood was calm, but there was something unfamiliar with the setting.

Keisha's eyes opened. While waiting for her pupils to dilate, she noticed the bed mattress felt unusually firm, unlike the soft, lumpy feeling it normally had, and for some strange reason, the sheets smelt of cologne. Keisha sluggishly raised her head. As she regained partial vision, she was able to make out the details of the room. The walls were different. They were painted an off shade of white instead of pink, and there were no pin-up posters covering them. Her portable stereo was missing, and the closet was on the opposite side of the room. Then it all made sense. Detroit never got around to taking her home last night; she was in his bedroom.

Keisha panicked. *Oh my God! What have I done?* She hesitantly peeped under the bed sheets, fearing the obvious. Yes, it was true; she was completely naked. Keisha sat up. The mixture of the restaurant wine and champagne was still in her system, and she had a buzz. She remembered Cece telling her about her first time. She staggered toward the adjoining bathroom, when she noticed a folded sheet of paper on the dresser that had her name written on it in bold print. She picked it up. It was a note from Detroit.

Good morning Beautiful,

You looked so peaceful when you were asleep that I couldn't bring myself to wake you. I've picked up all your clothes from the floor and laid them out on the chair, so you'll find them there. When you go into the bathroom, you'll find fresh linen on the towel rack and a clean robe hanging behind the door. Also, there's a brand-new toothbrush and a tube of paste on the sink. See you at breakfast.

Dee

Keisha looked at the chair sitting in the corner of the bedroom. Just as Detroit had described in the note, her clothes had been neatly laid out. When she walked into the bathroom, she found the items he had left on the towel rack and sink, as well. Keisha grabbed a handful of facial tissues from a box that sat on top of the toilet tank and then turned on the sink faucet. She gave the tissues a dab under the tap water and wiped the toilet seat before sitting on it. Her mother had taught her never to sit on anyone's toilet seat, especially if she didn't know the person well, but under the circumstances, this was an urgent matter. From the looks of it, Keisha need not worry because everything was clean and intact.

Damn, this place is spotless. He must have a maid come in once a week, she thought.

It didn't take long for Keisha to pass urine. She stood with her legs astride the toilet and looked down. There was a pinkish color in the bowl, just like Cece had told her. She stared at it for a few seconds and then flushed the tank. Keisha looked in the mirror. The image before her bared an uncanny likeness, but it lacked traits of her character. What she saw was the reflection of a promiscuous woman who engaged in casual sex with strange men.

Keisha felt that she had made a terrible mistake by sleeping with Detroit, and the guilty feeling confirmed her beliefs.

41

"No, you didn't, Keisha," she said, looking in the mirror.

But, it was now too late. Keisha was no longer a virgin; she had given Detroit a part of herself that she could never take back.

Keisha cupped her hands to her face and wept uncontrollably. She felt dirtier on the inside than she did on the surface. She turned the shower water on and stepped in the bathtub. Keisha opened a bar of soap and scrubbed vigorously at her skin, but the more she scrubbed, the more unclean she felt. She cried once more and prayed for strength. Finally, she managed to calm down and pull herself together.

Keisha re-entered the bedroom in a white terrycloth robe. There was still no sign of Detroit. She dug through her purse and located a small bottle of hand lotion, which she used to moisten her skin. As she sat on the bed, she thought about the events that led to her current situation. Maybe she had overreacted. After all, they were two consenting adults who made the decision to go further in their relationship.

She thought about her first sexual experience. An illustration played back in her mind with the graphics of an adult movie. A smile crept on Keisha's face as she remembered how forward and aggressive she had been. She also remembered how well Detroit handled his business. As Keisha thought back, she remembered there were a lot of females stalking him at the club. She now knew the reason why.

When Keisha got dressed, she walked out of the bedroom in search of Detroit. She found him sitting in the kitchen reading the morning paper.

"Well, good morning, sleeping beauty," he said humorously.

It was an awkward moment for Keisha. She stood with her head down, trying to avoid eye contact with Detroit. This was the first time she had seen him after being intimate last night, and she was embarrassed. She slowly lifted her head and took a seat next to him.

"Good morning," she said softly. "How long have you been up?"

"I get up at the crack of dawn, baby. I'm what you call an early riser, but I see you aren't." he answered.

"Please, don't even try it," Keisha said, now more relaxed. "You're the one who kept me up all night, remember? And let's not forget the fact that you got me drunk."

"I got you drunk? You were gulping those glasses of wine so fast that I lost count. Don't blame me if you can't hold your liquor," Detroit teased.

"First of all, I'll drink you under the table," Keisha said confidently. "And I counted five beers that you ordered before we even had dinner."

"Yeah, but I'm straight," Detroit replied, throwing his hands in the air with emphasis. "Now you, on the other hand, look like you could go for a cup of coffee."

"Whatever. Just make sure you put enough cream in my cup!" Keisha said.

"Didn't I give you enough cream last night?" Detroit replied humorously.

"You was alright, I guess," Keisha joked.

As Detroit got up to start the coffee, Keisha examined the apartment. She looked at the walls that had artistic paintings hanging on them. Then she noticed the furniture. Everything in the apartment looked as if it had just been unboxed, and it all appeared to be rather expensive. Keisha compared the plush Park Avenue apartment to her own home. She lived in a pretty decent neighborhood and had always felt she and her family lived comfortably. However, her house didn't stand a chance of winning any prize up against Detroit's place. Keisha thought of asking Detroit how he afforded to live such a lavish lifestyle on an accountant's salary. She assumed it was a rewarding career. But, to be honest, he was a black man living in a ritzy neighborhood with white people, and that was unheard of where she came from. It just didn't add up.

Detroit turned off the coffeemaker, got the silverware he needed, and took a seat beside Keisha. He prepared Keisha's cup just as she had asked and served it to her.

"Here you go, baby. One hot coffee with cream, just as you ordered," he said.

"Thanks. I owe you one," Keisha replied.

"Is that a promise?" Detroit asked. He moved in for a kiss, but Keisha backed off.

So, he proceeded to pour a cup for himself.

"Am I missing something here?" he asked. "You were all over me last night. Why the cold treatment now?"

"That's the whole point. Everything is moving too fast," Keisha said. "I mean, I lost my virginity to you last night, and I hardly know you. Then to top things off, I stayed out all night and didn't have the decency to call my folks. They're probably worried sick."

As Keisha began to cry again, Detroit stood up and drew a paper napkin from the utility drawer. He folded it into a square and knelt in front of her.

"I'm sorry, baby," he said apologetically, while wiping Keisha's tears. "I should have been more understanding. I realize that last night was your first time; this must be stressful on you. And as far as you staying out last night, I blame myself for that. I should have taken you home at a decent hour. But, to be totally honest, I'm glad I didn't. I've never felt for any woman the way I feel for you, Keisha. I'm in love with you," he said and gently stroked her cheekbone with his hand.

Detroit guided Keisha's lips to his and kissed her. Keisha didn't resist this time; she kissed him long and hard. Hearing him say the words "I Love You" was music to her soul. She was now convinced that she had given herself to the right man.

"I love you, too, Dee," she whispered before kissing him again.

Detroit lifted Keisha from the chair and carried her in his arms. Keisha stopped him when they got to the bedroom door.

"What are you doing?" she inquired, kissing him emphatically.

"I don't know, but do you want me to stop?" he asked between heavy breaths.

"You better not," she responded.

When they got inside the bedroom, they tore at each other's clothes like savages. Detroit and Keisha made love again and showered together afterwards. Keisha felt good about herself the second time around; she felt like a woman.

Chapter 8
Mama Knows Best

Keisha put her hands together and said a quick prayer. "I know I'm wrong for what I did last night, and I should have been more responsible. But, please, Lord, let Daddy be at work. Amen," she prayed and crossed her heart.

Taking a deep breath, she put the key in the door. It was well after ten in the morning, so there was no point in trying to sneak in quietly. Everyone would be awake by now. She braced herself and opened the door, ready to face the consequences. When she walked in, Victoria was standing in the hall with her arms folded. Keisha jumped and clutched at her chest when she saw her.

"Mama, you scared the mess out of me," she said. "Is Daddy here?" she asked quietly, looking around.

"Keisha, you know good and well that your father leaves out bright and early every morning to open the shop by eight o'clock. And you're lucky he isn't here," Victoria said, displeased.

"Did he say anything, Mama?" Keisha asked timidly.

"What was there to say, Keisha? I locked your bedroom door, leading him to believe that you were asleep. He doesn't know a thing yet."

"Whew." Keisha breathed a sigh of relief, and she kissed her mother on the cheek. "Thanks, Mama. You're the best," she said, then proceeded to walk past Victoria hurriedly.

Victoria grabbed hold of Keisha's arm, stopping her in her

tracks.

"Hold it right there, young lady!" she said, becoming more agitated. "You're not getting over that easy. I sat up half the night worrying about you, not knowing whether you were dead or alive. Now, if you think you're just going to waltz up in here like it's alright with no explanation, then you got another thing coming!"

Keisha knew her mother had every reason to be upset with her. She was completely wrong for not informing her of her whereabouts. But, after all she had been through during the past night and early morning, she was in no shape to be chastised. She tried reasoning with Victoria.

"Mama, I'm exhausted. Can we please talk about this later?" she begged.

Victoria had lost just about all of her patience with Keisha. Still holding onto her arm, she led Keisha to the dining room.

"Park it right there, and be quick about it!" she said with authority.

Keisha was sitting down before Victoria had finished her sentence.

"Keisha, you 'bout to work my last good nerve. Keep it up, and see if I don't slap the taste right out your mouth! I stood up for you, and I went against my husband by doing so. Is this your way of showing gratitude, by betraying my trust? I'm disappointed in you, Keisha. I thought you had better sense than this."

Victoria's words hit Keisha like a ton of bricks. Her mother always had her back when it came to giving her freedom. They had developed an honor of trust and never kept secrets from one another until now, and she had let her down. Keisha's eyes welled up with tears, and her lips trembled as she tried to get her words out.

"I am so sorry, Mama. Please forgive me. I never intended to hurt you or Daddy. I lost track of the time, and when I woke up this morning, I was too ashamed to call the house," she explained, bawling like a baby, and fell on Victoria's lap.

"Look at me, Keisha," Victoria ordered as Keisha lifted her head. "There's no point in you crying over spilled milk. What's done is done. I am upset, but don't ever feel like you can't come and talk to me. I'm still your mother, and I'll always be here for you no matter what. Your father may be stubborn at times, but he loves you, and we both want what's best. Now who is he?" she asked inquisitively.

Keisha looked at her mother as if she didn't have a clue what she was saying.

"Who is who, Mother?" she asked, dumbfounded.

"You know exactly what I mean, Keisha Johnson, and don't come at me with that "Mother" nonsense either," Victoria said with conviction. "You only call me that when you're trying to play up to me, and I see right through you. Besides, there ain't but one reason a girl could have for staying out like that. I may be getting old, but I'm not stupid!"

Keisha's face turned bright red. Her mother was nobody's fool. And how could she evade the question? It was already affirmed that she went out on a date last night. Therefore, bringing Cece into the equation was a no-no. She knew Victoria wouldn't budge until she got a direct answer from her, so she confessed.

"It was Alvin, Mama. He called last night when you answered the telephone, remember?" she said, trembling.

"What you shaking for, girl? I'm not gonna hit you. I'm just getting comfortable," Victoria said, pulling her seat closer. "So tell me, just how long have you known this "friend," and how long have you been sexually active? Don't lie to me either!"

Keisha knew she would only have upset Victoria more if she were to tell her the whole truth about what happened. She had to admit that she indulged; that was unquestionable. But, there was no way on earth she would ever admit to sleeping with a man whom she had only met a week ago. So, she fabricated her story a bit.

"Alvin and I have been seeing each other for a couple of months now. I should have told you about him before, but I wasn't sure where our relationship was going at first. I had to make sure he was the right one before I brought him home to meet the family. We've only done it once, and that was last night. But, I do love him, Mama, and he loves me."

Victoria walked to the stove and returned with a teakettle filled with hot water. Keisha went to the cupboards and got the tea bags, cups, and saucers for them. Victoria spoke as she poured the water.

"Keisha," she began, "you are far too young to even think about being in love at your age. What you're feeling right now is lust."

"That's not true, Mama," Keisha responded, cutting Victoria short. "I really do love—"

"Excuse me. Did you hear me say that I was finished?" Victoria snapped.

"No, ma'am. I'm sorry."

"Don't be sorry. Just sit there and listen," Victoria demanded. "Keisha, I've watched you grow from a little girl into a beautiful young woman, and I have always been very proud of you. But, I think you're making a big mistake by diving head first into a relationship with this Alvin person," she said sincerely. "Now, I'm not going to tell you what to do, but I will give you some words of advice. You have such a bright future ahead of you, Keisha. Don't go burning your bridges until you've crossed that road. I want you to promise me something."

"Yes, Mama. What is it?" Keisha asked.

Victoria paused and gazed into Keisha's eyes with concern.

"I want you to promise me that you'll be careful. But most of all, follow your heart."

"Don't worry, Mama, I promise to be careful," she replied and hugged Victoria.

The telephone rang, interrupting the shared moment. Victoria got up.

"Answer the phone, Keisha. It's probably for you anyway. That girl Cece has been calling all morning. We'll talk more about this later on," she said, then walked into her bedroom.

Keisha was exhausted. The last thing she needed right then was to gossip with Cece, especially since she'd just been chewed out by her mother. Yet, she reluctantly answered the phone.

"Hello," she said unenthusiastically.

"Well, well, well, if it isn't little Ms. Goody Two Shoes. So you finally decided to come home, huh?" Cece cracked.

"Cece, shut up and mind your own business. I'm not in a playing mood right now."

"Keisha, I don't know who you think you're talking to, but you better back that shit up! When your mom said you weren't home, I didn't know what to think. For all I knew, you could have been kidnapped or strangled to death. You better tell me something!"

"Damn, does everyone think I'm incapable of taking care of myself? You know I was with Detroit, Cece. I called and told you myself. What, you got amnesia all of a sudden?" Keisha said, now frustrated.

"Oh, so it's like that? You got a man now, so you just gonna drop me, right? I never thought you would let some lame-ass nigga come between our friendship, Keisha. We've been girls forever. But you know what? Fuck you and him. When that motherfucker leaves you…and he will…I want you to remember exactly what you just said!" Cece exclaimed, hot tempered.

"Hold up, Cece. I ain't mean to come at you like that." Keisha felt sorry about speaking to her best friend in such a way. "I know you were just concerned and looking out. We good?"

"Yeah, we good," Cece answered as she cooled off. "I'm sorry for screaming on you, too. Now, since we all good and shit, tell me where your ass was last night?"

Keisha walked to the hall to see if Victoria was around. When she saw that she wasn't, she continued the conversation.

"I spent the night at Detroit's apartment, and guess what? We did it!" she announced proudly.

"I knew it! I knew it," Cece proclaimed. "I knew you were going to let him be your first by the way you kept talking about him. I wish I would have said something to you about it, but I didn't. So, how was it? Did it hurt, or did you like it?"

"Well, it was a little bit of both," Keisha admitted. "At first, I couldn't wait for it to be over, but then, I started to like it and didn't want him to stop."

"Well, I'll be damned; my girl Keisha is a full-fledged woman. Welcome to the other side," Cece exaggerated. "You can hang it up now. Your peeps ain't falling no more for that innocent role you be frontin'. What did they have to say?"

"My father doesn't know, and hopefully, he never will," Keisha confided. "But, my mother was cool about it, surprisingly."

"Yeah, your mom is pretty cool about stuff. Sometimes I wish we could trade mothers, 'cause mine is too old fashioned," Cece admitted.

"Nah, that's alright. My mama got all her teeth, and she don't smell like Ben-Gay," Keisha said jokingly.

"You know what? Jahlil could use a shape-up. I wonder if your father's chair is open."

"Okay, you got me on that one," Keisha admitted.

"That's what I thought, smart-ass," Cece replied.

During the months ahead, Keisha ran a hectic schedule. Going to school and working at the supermarket demanded most of her time, and now Detroit was added to the agenda, which made the situation more complicated. Still, Keisha managed to balance them all adequately and didn't mind because she was in love.

Detroit had introduced Keisha to a world she never knew existed, and she was on cloud nine. Quiet romantic dinners, lavish shopping sprees, and even the little things like holding hands while walking in the park, were the rewards of Keisha's labor.

The relationship flourished, but sadly, Keisha's life took a drastic turn. She watched as her world began to crumble.

Chapter 9
New York's Finest

It was a brisk, windy day in autumn. The fallen leaves had blown against the sidewalk curbs and were piled in the sewer gutters. The No. 2 and 3 New Lots Avenue bound subway trains sped past every few minutes as they pulled into the Saratoga Avenue station above, leaving a deafening roar that drowned out every sound below as it left the platform. Pedestrians hurried along the busy streets to escape the nipping cold weather, while a handful of winos kept themselves warm by hovering around a burning steel drum filled with wood and other leftover fragments of the dilapidated building that stood behind them.

Detectives John O'Reilly and Harry Flanagan pulled up in a police surveillance van and parked directly across the street from First Stop, the storefront name for Percy Solomon's numbers hole. O'Reilly was a stout, grey-haired, fifty-year-old Irish cop who had been on the force for twenty years. Flanagan was a thirty-year-old, clean-cut rookie with a sharp nose, who had just completed training. This was his first day on the job.

O'Reilly's previous partner had been killed six months ago during a routine stop for a license check. He was assigned to desk duty for a grievance period while he coped with personal issues. O'Reilly wasn't thrilled when his superior assigned Flanagan as his new partner. He stated the rookie lacked in experience and would only slow him down. In any case, the decision was final, and they became a team.

O'Reilly reached into a white paper bag and fished out two jelly doughnuts and a hot cup of coffee in a Styrofoam cup. He devoured the food while Flanagan flipped through the report to get a feel of the assignment. It was clear he didn't rank on O'Reilly's Top Ten list of favorite people, so Flanagan kept silent and spoke only when it was necessary. However, seeing that his partner had no intensions of being professional, Flanagan took matters into his own hands to break the ice.

"So what's the deal on the suspect?" he inquired casually.

With food still in his mouth, O'Reilly turned his head. "It's all there in the report, in black and white. Didn't you read your copy?" he asked.

"As a matter of fact, I did," Flanagan replied. "I just thought you'd be able to enlighten me with hands-on experience. I understand you handled the case for a substantial period with your last colleague."

Flanagan had touched a nerve. O'Reilly suffered from depression dealing with the loss of his longtime friend, partly because he felt responsible for his death. O'Reilly was asleep in an unmarked car when his former partner, Detective Patrick Doyle, needed him most. Doyle was shot in the head and died instantly as he approached three Chicano youths for a busted taillight. O'Reilly underwent psychiatric therapy and relied heavily on prescription drugs as a result of the trauma he sustained.

"You don't know anything rookie. You're still wet behind the ears," he grunted. "I'm already starting not to like you, so kissing up to me ain't gonna work. And keep my partner's name out of your mouth. You're supposed to be taking notes, so watch and observe!"

"That's it. I've had it up to here with your tough guy act," Flanagan stated. "I don't like this setup any more than you do, but this is as good as it's going to get. We're stuck with each other. The sooner you accept that, the better off the both of us will be!"

O'Reilly was stunned. This was the first time Flanagan had shown any sign of backbone since they first teamed up. *The kid just might work out after all,* he thought.

"It took a lot of balls for you to stand up to me like that, rookie. I respect that. We're getting somewhere now. So you want to learn the ropes, do you? Well then, I'm going to give it to you straight."

"Thank you, sir, and I didn't mean to be so harsh. I was totally out of character, and it will never happen again." Flanagan responded.

"Now you're starting to sound like a pussy again. Don't make me change my mind, rookie. I was just about to give you the benefit of the doubt, so don't be a wimp."

"Yes, sir, and the name's Harry."

"Fine, Harry, and from now on, you can call me John. Now, let's get down to business."

O'Reilly sat his coffee cup in a holder and picked up the rap sheet. He browsed through it momentarily. He had probably read the document more than a hundred times before. This had been his case before the chief restricted him to the office. O'Reilly sat behind the desk for three years with other agents who were either in the same predicament or too old to be out in the field because they had reached the retirement mark.

Flanagan sat right at his side, but he trusted him as far as he could see him. O'Reilly despised new rookies. If it were left up to him, he would have worked the case alone.

"So, Flanagan, tell me what you know already."

Flanagan smiled with confidence. He had been up all night studying the case and was craving to assert his expertise.

"The suspect's name is Percy Solomon," Flanagan stated. "He originated from New Orleans, Louisiana. His father was a Spanish merchant, and his mother was a Creole woman. He moved to Harlem, New York, in his early twenties and started out as a runner for a racket banker affiliated with one of the most powerful mafia outfits in the city. The guy that Solomon worked for used to own this place," he said, pointing to the storefront. "With a flair for figures and the money he saved, Solomon leased the store after the coloreds dominated the inner city and whites fled to the suburbs. When he established himself, Solomon purchased the business and branched out. Besides the storefront, he also owns a nightclub."

O'Reilly gave Flanagan a look of approval. "Well now, it looks like you've done your homework. There's not much more I can say. You've covered it all."

"Thanks, O'Reilly. I am totally intrigued by this case. But, tell me, you've been tracking him for a long time. Why now?" Flanagan asked.

"You know how it is, son. We have to go by the book," O'Reilly explained.

However, there was one miscellaneous piece of information that he purposely left out. O'Reilly was on the payroll and muscling Percy for more money. When Percy refused to pay the increase, O'Reilly pursued him with a vengeance.

"You're right. How could I be so dumb?" Flanagan responded, slapping himself lightly across the forehead.

"The only dumb questions are the ones you don't ask," O'Reilly stated. "You remember that, kid. It'll take you a long way."

O'Reilly picked up his radio and sent Flanagan to throw out the leftover trash from lunch. He called in for back-up from the 73rd Precinct. Within minutes, three responding units pulled up. O'Reilly gave Flanagan a nod.

"Okay, kid, it's time for us to move in," he said.

"I'm ready when you are," Flanagan replied.

O'Reilly and Flanagan hopped out of the vehicle and ran towards the store with their guns cocked at their sides. Two officers were already securing the front of the building. One man stood on either side of the door. Another set of officers blocked the streets off and directed the spectators that had gathered around to clear the area. The remaining officers guarded the back door.

Inside the store, Percy, Detroit, and Moe awaited the officers' entrance. Moe had spotted the unmarked van when it pulled up and parked at the corner, so he warned the others. Percy had already made preparations for the bust. He knew it was just a matter of time before O'Reilly stabbed him in the back after he refused to pay the bribery money.

Percy called his wife and told her where he had stashed a sum of money for his bail. He had her take the money and stay with a close relative until he gave her further notice. Detroit stacked all the account books in a portable safe and hid it in a floorboard under one of the refrigerated coolers. Moe kept himself busy collecting all the betting slips that he could find. Then he cut them into tiny pieces with a pair of scissors and flushed as many as he could down the toilet.

Suddenly, the door was kicked in. It flew into the wall, knocking over a magazine stand that stood nearby. Two of the officers rushed in, waving their guns and pointing them at the three men.

"Police!" one of them yelled. "Put your hands above your heads and slowly step forward!"

Percy, Moe, and Detroit calmly responded to the officer's orders and stepped forward.

"What in the hell is going on here?" Percy asked. "You don't just barge into a man's place of business unannounced. Do you motherfuckers even have a warrant?"

Just then, Detectives O'Reilly and Flanagan entered. O'Reilly unfolded a document that he was holding and approached Percy.

"I'm glad you asked," O'Reilly said boastfully. He held the paper up for Percy to read. "Percy Solomon, you are under arrest for extortion and the illegal distribution of alcohol."

"That's bullshit! You got nothing on me, O'Reilly!"

"Tell it to the judge, Solomon. Remember that nice little nightclub of yours over on Tapscott Street? Well, it's been shut down. Maybe that'll refresh your memory. Cuff him," O'Reilly ordered, addressing the officers. "And take these two as accomplices."

"This will never stand up in court, you pasty son of a bitch. You can't arrest me without evidence. You set me up!"

"My apologies to ya, nigger," O'Reilly said, tipping his hat.

"I got your nigger right here, you flat-footed pig!" Percy shouted. "I'll see you in court!"

"You'll be seeing me before your court date. You can bet on it. Get it? Bet-on-it!" O'Reilly cracked a smirk as the men were led out.

The rest of the officers ransacked the store, destroying most of the merchandise as they confiscated evidence.

Down at the station, the suspects were fingerprinted, taken for mug shots, and then booked. Later that afternoon, O'Reilly and Flanagan conducted an official interrogation on all three men. Detroit was the first to be interviewed. He was taken to a dim box-shaped room, where he sat at a small square table with O'Reilly while Flanagan paced the floor.

"Cigarette?" O'Reilly offered, taking a pack from his shirt pocket.

"Thanks. I could use one," Detroit said, taking the smoke.

After giving him a light, O'Reilly started the questioning.

"Tell me, son, you look like an intelligent young man. How did you get mixed up with the likes of Solomon, the scum of the earth?"

Detroit took a drag of the cigarette. "Please enlighten me as to what you mean by scum of the earth, detective," he responded, exhaling a narrow chain of smoke. "Mr. Solomon has always been a fair employer, at least to my understanding."

O'Reilly stood up. "Don't be giving me any trouble, you beige piece of shit!" he said, smacking the bulb of the swag light that hung over the table.

Flanagan rushed over to restrain the older detective from getting physical.

"Calm down, John," he said, patting him on the shoulder. "It's been a long day for us all. Let me take over for a stint."

"Maybe that's a good idea, but I'm watching you!" O'Reilly warned Detroit and then took a seat beside him.

"Okay, I'll take it from here," Flanagan said. Once he sat down, the interview went at a steadier pace.

"So, Mr. Williams, what is your association to Solomon?"

"He's my employer, of course. I handle all of Mr. Solomon's financial matters."

"Have you noticed any suspicious activity going on around the store? I mean, anything out of the ordinary?"

"No, I haven't noticed a thing. Not since I've been there, anyway."

"And how long have you been employed by Mr. Solomon?"

"Not very long. A little over a year."

"Okay, Mr. Williams, you're free to go."

"Just like that?" Detroit asked, surprised.

"Just like that," Flanagan replied. "Of course, there's some paperwork you'll have to fill out, but you're a free man after that. We appreciate your cooperation."

An officer was called into the room and escorted Detroit out. Infuriated, O'Reilly confronted Flanagan.

"What was that? We could have gotten more information out of him, and you let him go. I should have never listened to you, rookie!"

"There's no use in getting upset, John," Flanagan said. "According to the report, there was no reason to withhold him. He doesn't even have a track record."

Flanagan was right. The only reason Detroit was brought in was because O'Reilly included him as an aided accomplish. In fact, the whole raid at the store was a hoax. O'Reilly hadn't gotten the clear to close in on the gambling investigation, because there wasn't enough factual evidence to prove the case. He had sent Flanagan to throw out the leftover trash to distract him, and while Flanagan was gone, he called in and reported a robbery at the storefront. However, the warrant that O'Reilly had was official. Percy was illegally selling alcohol in the nightclub.

It was a Friday afternoon, so Percy would not be released until he appeared before a judge the following Monday. Moe had warrants for refusing to appear in court for beating up on his ex-wife, so he would spend time in jail, as well.

Chapter 10
Double Trouble

After completing a long list of forms, Detroit was dismissed of all charges and released from the precinct that afternoon. The arrest was a big wakeup call. It made him realize how dangerous it was being affiliated to the underworld, and no job was worth him risking his life.

Detroit wanted to beat himself in the head for being so gullible. He thought back and remembered how simple life used to be. Only a year ago, he had a rewarding career as a broker for a prominent mortgage firm. He worked a 9 to 5 shift, Monday through Friday, and came home every night to a tiny sublet room for a nice cold beer and a heated TV dinner. It wasn't the most exciting life, but then again, he didn't have to look over his shoulder every minute of the day. That all changed when Percy Solomon walked into the office and made him an offer he couldn't refuse.

While purchasing his new home, Percy noticed how fast and precise the young man was at handling figures. After a little persuasion and a generous salary offer, Percy talked Detroit into leaving his job to work for him managing his books at the nightclub. Detroit was good at cutting corners, and Percy gained revenue from his expertise. Percy admired Detroit's work ethic and saw him as a younger version of himself. Not long after, Percy took Detroit under his wing and brought him into the numbers game, making him second in command of the operation.

Detroit thought about his future. It was nothing but luck that he escaped facing jail time. It was time to get out, and he knew it. He had seen a number of headstrong fools go down by refusing to go with their instincts, and he wasn't about to become another statistic. It was now or never.

Moe was next to be questioned, and finally, they called Percy into the room. Percy became suspicious when he returned to his cell and saw that Detroit had not returned, especially since he was the first one to go in the interrogation room. *Something ain't right,* he thought, and then called Moe over to the corner of the cell for a meeting.

"The line has gotten shorter over here, hasn't it?" he said.

"It sure does seem that way, boss," Moe agreed. "What you think about that?"

"Well, it seems to me that our friend has either forgotten his way back to the cell, or he's traded to another team without telling us," Percy stated bluntly.

"What you mean by that, boss? You don't think he said anything, do you?" Moe asked. He began sweating profusely with fear.

"Look around. You don't see him, do you? I'd say there's a rat that needs to be exterminated," Percy responded.

"Are you sure about that, boss? I mean, the kid has been around us for a while, and he's always been loyal. Do you think he would be fool enough to cross you? He knows you can get to him from the inside."

"I wouldn't say it hasn't crossed my mind," Percy told him. "You know, I treated him like a son and made him my protégé; taught him everything he knows. At one point, I would have trusted him with my own life. I hope I'm wrong, but there's only one way to find out."

"Whatchu gonna do, boss?" Moe asked.

"I need to get to a phone. I am entitled to one call," Percy said.

"I'll be back in a minute."

Percy called out to one of the guards patrolling the cellblock and asked to make the call. On the way to the phone, he inquired about the whereabouts of the friend who came in with him.

The guard informed Percy that Detroit's charges had been dropped and that he was on his way to being released.

Once Percy made his call, he was returned to the cell. Moe could tell something was wrong by the look on his face.

"So what's the verdict, boss?" he asked.

"It's just as I thought. There's a big rat running loose in the city," Percy replied. "I just got the word from the flat foot that let me out."

"I don't believe it, boss. I never made the kid out for a snitch. I guess that saying is true. Keep your enemies close and your friends closer."

"That's true, Moe, but I go by another credo," Percy said. "If you fuck with the bull, you get the horns!"

*****

Detroit stepped out of the precinct carrying a small envelope with his belongings inside. After all the hell he'd gone through, he was ready to call it a day and go home, but his car was still parked at the storefront. The worst part of the day was over. All he had to do now was get his ride and never look back again.

He opened the envelope and reached inside it for his wallet, only to discover that a hundred dollar bill was missing. Luckily for him, the thief was kind enough to leave twenty dollars for cab fare.

Spotting a payphone on the corner, Detroit walked to it and opened the phone directory that was tied to the shelf. As he flipped through the pages, two identical-looking black males who appeared to be in their early twenties pulled up in a black Mustang. It was Dru and Cyrus a.k.a. The Twinz. They were average in size and height, but feared in the streets for their ruthless nature. Dru and Cyrus filled in as bouncers at the nightclub on weekends, but they were also Percy's personal bodyguards. They got out of the car and moved to each side of Detroit, who nodded his head to greet them.

"What's up, Dru...Cyrus. What y'all doing around these neck of the woods?" he asked, sensing trouble.

"We saw what happened on the news, man. We came down to see if we could be of any help," Cyrus answered. "But, it looks like you made out alright."

"Yeah, man, ain't that something? I wasn't prepared for any shit like this to happen. I just got cut. They asked me a few questions and let me go."

"Is that so?" Dru asked. "Well, you must have sang like a canary, because we just got a call from Percy on the inside, and they ain't letting him or Moe out no time soon."

"So what are you trying to say, Dru? You think I snitched? C'mon, man, you know me better than that."

"I'm saying, Percy got this big-time lawyer that couldn't do nothing for him, and here you are walking free. The shit just don't look right."

"I don't give a fuck what it looks like," Detroit stated angrily. "And unless you've forgotten, both of you work under me, so I ain't telling you shit. We'll resolve this issue when Percy gets out. But, until then, back the fuck up!"

"I can't do that, partner," Dru said arrogantly. "You see, there's been a change of plans. I just got a call from Percy, and you've been demoted in rank. So, until he gets out, that makes me the head nigga in charge!"

Detroit knew that Dru was probably telling the truth, but he tried to buy himself some time.

"What? I don't believe you," he said, sounding surprised.

"That's right. I'm running the show now, whether you believe it or not," Dru told him. "Now get ya ass in the car. We're going

65

for a little ride!"

Detroit looked at Dru and Cyrus, weighing his options. He was about to make a run for it, but Dru caught onto him.

"Nigga, don't even think about it," he said in a cocky tone. "We figured you might think of trying some heroic shit, so we brought a little negotiator to help you decide if you wanna be brave or not." Dru tapped Cyrus on the shoulder. "Yo, let him see it, son," he said, folding his arms.

Cyrus pulled his leather blazer to the side, exposing the shiny barrel of a .38 revolver that was tucked in his waist. Getting the message, Detroit got in the car.

"This nigga ain't as dumb as we thought," Cyrus commented, while shoving Detroit's head down so he wouldn't hit his head as he got in. He sat beside Detroit in the back with his finger on the trigger and waited for Dru to get behind the steering wheel.

Detroit sat silently as they drove off. He had never been more terrified in his life than he was at that moment. *How the fuck did I get myself into this shit? There's gotta be a way out,* he thought. Detroit knew he was living on borrowed time, and he had to act fast. He turned to face the window as he devised a plan to escape from his adversaries.

*****

The evening sky was silhouetted by the shade of night. Dru eased his foot from the gas pedal as he turned the car into an alley behind a pizzeria on Dumont Avenue. In a desperate attempt, Detroit delivered two lightning quick strikes that land directly on the bridge of Cyrus's nose, shattering it in three places. A dazed Cyrus shrieked in agonizing pain and grabbed at his nose, which was now oozing with blood. Detroit lunged for the gun, which was still in Cyrus's possession. A struggle commenced, and two shots were fired. Cyrus was too slow. Blood gushed from his opened torso; he slumped over and dropped his head. Dru slammed on the brakes, swerved the car into a brick wall.

"Yo, what the fuck is going on back there?" he yelled out, then looked over his shoulder to see his dead brother lying in the back seat.

Normally, Dru carried his strap with him, but he left it behind this time because he figured Detroit would be light work. With his hands trembling with fear, Dru managed to get the car door open and quickly dashed out. Detroit seized the bloody gun from Cyrus's limp body and ran after Dru. He aimed and fired a shot, hitting Dru in the lower spine. Dru fell to the ground, screaming in anguish. Detroit watched as Dru crawled on his stomach like a snake. Then he kicked him in the side and rolled him onto his back using the heel of his shoe.

Dru looked up, and spitting blood from his mouth, he said, "Whatchu waiting for muthafucka? Kill me!"

"It'll be my pleasure," Detroit answered. "But, just for the record, I never snitched on anybody, you ignorant sonofabitch!"

He fired another shot, hitting Dru's skull. Fragments of bone and minced flesh splattered onto Detroit's shoes.

He ran back to the car, kicked Cyrus's corpse out, and jumped behind the wheel. He drove cautiously until he stopped a block away from the storefront and abandoned the car in an empty lot. He wiped his fingerprints off the gun with a handkerchief and tossed it into a sewer drain. Then he ran down the next block.

When Detroit reached the storefront, he got into his own car and drove uptown to his apartment. He quickly stuffed as much of his clothing and personal belongings that he can fit into a suitcase. Next, he retrieved a metal box from the closet, which contained a hundred and twenty-five thousand dollars inside.

As Detroit rushed out the door, he bumped into his landlord, Francesco, in the hall.

Francesco looked down at the luggage that Detroit was

carrying.

"What is this? You aren't leaving us, are you?" he asked.

"No, I'm just going on a little business trip, Francesco," Detroit replied. "I'll be back."

Chapter 11
Going My Way

Keisha came home from work that evening to find everyone crowded in front of the television set in the family room.

"What's going on?" she asked, entering the room.

"Yo, they just busted First Stop over on Saratoga Avenue!" her brother T.J. said. "They got Moe, too. It's been all over the news!"

"I don't care what happens to those other two bums, but it's a shame that Moe was involved," Thomas said. "He only works at the nightclub for that man as a means to get by. He lost his job right after he got locked up for getting into trouble with his wife, Eloise. How else was he supposed to survive? I feel sorry for him."

Keisha looked on as the news reporter described the crime scene in full detail.

"Police arrested three men today at First Stop grocery store located on Saratoga Avenue. The owner, Percy Solomon, was taken in for suspicion of conducting an illegal gambling operation on the premises. Solomon is the owner of a prestigious nightclub called The Mixer, which was also temporarily shut down today for the illegal sale of alcoholic beverages. Two other suspects, Morris Brown and Alvin Williams, were taken in for questioning."

Keisha gasped as she watched Detroit being taken into custody. The man who she thought she knew and had fallen madly in love with was nothing more than a common criminal. Every word he had said to her was a lie. Their whole relationship was built on a lie. Tears of hurt and betrayal began to swell up in Keisha's eyes. She turned around and ran out the front door.

"Keisha, come back here! Where are you going?" Victoria yelled.

"What's wrong with that girl now?" Thomas asked.

Neither Keisha nor Victoria had mentioned a word about Keisha dating Detroit to Thomas, and luckily for them, they hadn't. Thomas would have had a fit if he knew his only daughter was seeing an older man and a criminal to say the least.

"Oh, it's nothing important," Victoria said. "She must have forgotten to bring home the groceries I asked her to get for me."

"She gets that upset over groceries? Vicky, I'm beginning to wonder about our daughter. I always thought Jr. was the crazy one."

"Oh hush, Thomas," Victoria said, hitting him lightly on the arm.

*****

Keisha ran down the street at top speed not knowing which way she was going, and she didn't care. The only thing she was certain of was that she wanted to get away from everyone and be alone.

Detroit sat parked in his car a few doors down from where Keisha lived. Keisha was so upset that she didn't see him there and ran right past him. Detroit honked at Keisha, but she still didn't acknowledge him, so he hit the gas and tailed her.

He honked again as he drove up. Keisha slowed down and turned to see who was honking. When she saw Detroit, she picked up her pace and kept going.

"Keisha!" he called out, but she paid him no mind. "Keisha! Come on, baby. We need to talk."

"Stay away from me, you liar! I have nothing to say to you!" she screamed.

Detroit got out of the car and caught Keisha by the arm.

"I can tell from your reaction that you already know. But, I can explain, Keisha," he said.

"Take your hands off me!" she yelled, shaking him loose. "There's nothing to explain, Dee. I saw it all on the news. I gave my heart to you. How could you lie to me? Everything about you is a damn lie!" she said tearfully, while beating her fist into his chest.

He grabbed Keisha and held onto her.

"I know, baby. I know," he said, resting his chin on her head. "I hate myself for lying to you, Keisha, but I had no choice. My hands were tied. It was the only way to protect you."

Keisha had mixed feelings. She had every right to hate Detroit for misleading her, but her feelings for him could not be denied. She was still madly in love with him.

Keisha looked up into Detroit's eyes and nearly melted in his arms.

"You said you loved me. Did you mean it, or was that another one of your lies?" she asked emotionally.

"Keisha, I love you more than you could ever imagine. That's why I'm here," he said, kissing her softly. "I want to spend the rest of my life with you."

Keisha got excited. "Are you asking me to marry you?"

"Yes...well, not right away, but eventually," Detroit replied.

"Then what are you asking me? I don't understand."

"I've made far too many mistakes, Keisha. It's time I close the book on this chapter in my life and start a new one. I'm going away, and I want you to come with me."

"You're confusing me, Dee," Keisha said. "Why do we have to go anywhere, and where would we go?" she asked.

"I'm not sure, but it doesn't matter as long as we're together. Keisha, I have to be honest. I know too much. Percy would never let me walk away freely. That's why we have to leave now. It's too dangerous to stay here," Detroit told her, hiding the fact that Percy had a hit out for him.

"Dee, you know that I love you, and I want nothing more than to be with you, but my life is here. I haven't finished school, and what about my family? How can I leave them behind?"

"Baby, you can still finish school somewhere else. And it's not like I'm asking you to desert your family. You can keep in touch. Hell, we can come back to visit when this blows over."

Keisha's demeanor changed abruptly. *This can't be happening to me,* she thought. But, there was no doubt in what was happening. Keisha's life with Detroit had come to an end.

"I'm sorry, Dee, but I can't do this. Please don't make me choose..."

Detroit silenced her words with a kiss.

"I'm sorry, too, baby," he said, then got back in the car.

Keisha ran up to Detroit as he started the ignition. She tapped on the window as the engine geared.

"Wait, Dee. You don't have to go. We'll work this out together somehow," she told him, now in tears.

Detroit lowered the window on his side.

"Goodbye, Keisha," he said one last time before driving away.

Keisha kept her eyes on Detroit until the car faded out of sight.

Chapter 12

Growing Pains

Keisha was emotionally distraught after her break up with Detroit. She became depressed, and the next couple of weeks were trying times for her. She stopped attending classes at school, and the supermarket let her go for getting too many write-ups. Her body also went through changes. She lost her appetite. Then, when she did try to eat something, she couldn't keep anything down. Some days were so difficult that Keisha barely found the strength to lift her head from the pillow. She spent most of her time lying in bed, staring at the ceiling.

Concerned for her daughter's health, Victoria intervened one morning and took Keisha to the emergency room at Kings County Hospital. After a long wait, Keisha was taken into a room to have her vital signs checked by one of the triage nurses. Her vital signs appeared to be normal, but the doctor who treated her ran some tests using blood and urine samples just to be safe. Twenty minutes later, the doctor returned to the room carrying Keisha's chart under his arm. Keisha and Victoria sat at the edge of their seats in anticipation, waiting to hear the results.

"Well, Ms. Johnson, it looks like we have good news," he started, opening the chart. "All of the tests came back negative. There were no abnormalities in your blood glucose or cholesterol levels. However, your blood pressure was a little high. Does anyone in the family have a history of hypertension?" he asked.

Victoria and Keisha looked at one another with the mutual urge to slap the doctor into the next room for keeping them in suspense. But, they held back from doing so.

"No one that I can recall," Keisha replied.

"Not from my side of the family," Victoria added. "But, she recently broke up with her boyfriend, and she isn't handling it very well. That's our main concern, Doctor."

"That would explain it," the doctor said. "There are other resources in our facility where you can get additional help, Ms. Johnson. After all, we can't expect to have a healthy baby if the mother isn't healthy."

Keisha's jaw dropped, and Victoria nearly fell out the chair. Keisha was experiencing several different symptoms at the same time, but they were all relevant to her emotional stress from breaking up with Detroit, or at least that's what she thought. The news of the pregnancy came as a big shock.

"What baby? Who said anything about a baby? I'm not pregnant!" she argued.

"Did you just say the word *baby*?" Victoria asked, making sure she heard correctly.

"Yes. Ms. Johnson is six weeks pregnant, but I assumed that you already knew. Please excuse me for breaking the news to you this way."

"There's no need to apologize, Doctor. You are only doing your job. But, I must say this is quite a shock to us," Victoria admitted.

"The important thing to do in this situation is to stay calm, for both the mother and baby," the doctor said. "Now that we've detected the pregnancy, we'll see what we can do about getting her the proper prenatal care that she needs and a specialist for the mental disorder."

Keisha jumped off the examination table with a burst of energy. She grabbed her purse from the desk and got in the doctor's face.

"Hold up. First of all, you don't even know me like that. How you just gonna come up in here and call somebody crazy? What you need to do is take your old ass back to the lab and run these tests again, 'cause I ain't pregnant!"

"Keisha, where are your manners? You have no right to speak to the doctor that way. He's only doing what's best for you and the baby," Victoria said, then turned to the physician. "Please excuse my daughter's behavior, sir. She's having a rough time right now. I'm sure you can understand."

"I fully understand, Mrs. Johnson," he said. "Wow, this is more serious than I thought. She sure is a feisty one! Please calm her down, or we'll have to sedate her and keep her overnight for observation. By the way, does she have her own gynecologist?"

"His name is Dr. Fitzgerald, and he works here in the hospital," Victoria answered.

"Yes, Dr. Fitzgerald is a fine doctor," the doctor said. "I'll send him an update on Keisha's chart, and I want her to see him as soon as possible. In the meantime, I'll get you the information you need for the other thing. I'll be right back," he told them.

Victoria shut the door when the doctor left the room. She was about to snatch Keisha by the collar, but she held back for the baby's sake.

"Keisha, what in the world has gotten into you? Cussing at that man like that with your foul mouth," she said. "If you embarrass me one more time, they will be keeping your behind here tonight!"

"I'm sorry, Mama. Too many things are happening all at once, and I'm scared. What am I going to do?" Keisha asked, sobbing.

"Keisha, I warned you about this. Now didn't I? Ain't no point in you crying about it now. You've got to be strong for this child you're carrying inside of you," Victoria said, feeling Keisha's abdomen. "I can't get over this. I'm going to be a grandmother! And Thomas is...oh my Lord!" She stopped abruptly. "Keisha, your father is going to hit the ceiling when he finds out about this!"

"Do we have to tell Daddy right now, Mama? I mean, shouldn't we wait until the timing is right?"

"And when will that be, Keisha? The day he walks in the house and sees you with a big belly? We are not hiding anything from your father anymore. When he comes home tonight, you're going to tell him everything!"

"Yes, ma'am," Keisha answered. "But will you help me, please?"

"You are on your own this time, girl. You've already got me involved enough in this mess. Don't you worry any about your father, though. I'll take care of him. But, this is the last time, Keisha."

"Thanks, Mama. I knew I could count on you." Keisha gave her a hug.

A few minutes later, the doctor returned to the room.

"Here you are, Ms. Johnson," he said, handing Keisha a form with the names of various psychiatrists. "Now make sure you call at least one of them when you get home. Good luck."

"Thank you, Doctor. I will do that as soon as I get home," Keisha said.

However, when Keisha got outside, she crumpled the paper into a ball and tossed it in the trash.

Chapter 13

Kick Rocks

Anyone who knew Thomas Johnson also knew that he had a healthy appetite. When Keisha and Victoria left the hospital, they went to the supermarket to pick up groceries for dinner. That afternoon, they prepared barbequed spareribs, baked macaroni and cheese, and fresh-cut green beans. It was Thomas's favorite meal. Of course, this wasn't going to stop him from being upset once he found out about the new addition to the family. However, it gave them enough ammunition to ease into the topic before breaking the news to him. If the dinner didn't go well, Victoria had a backup plan. A little personal time before bed always did the trick.

Thomas stepped in the house around 5:30 p.m. He usually stayed at the barbershop until closing and locked up himself, but he got into an argument earlier with a customer who brought her son in for a cut. The mother complained that the haircut was uneven, and refused to pay the bill. Thomas personally cut the boy's hair himself, so it was only natural that the woman's comment ticked him off. He retaliated by saying the boy's head was so nappy that it broke the teeth in his Afro pick when he combed through it. The woman stormed out of the shop without paying, and Thomas's nerves were so bad that he didn't touch another head for the rest of the day.

Victoria met Thomas at the door when he came in.

"You're home early," she said with a big embrace.

"Yeah, I had to get out of there before I hurt somebody. It sure smells good up in here. What you burning?"

"Hi, Daddy," Keisha interrupted. "We made all of your favorites: ribs, mac-n-cheese, and green beans. And for dessert, sweet potato pie and vanilla ice cream."

"So what's the occasion?" Thomas asked. "It's not my birthday, and I know that Jr. hasn't moved out. I smelled his feet out in the hall when I came up the stairs."

Victoria and Keisha laughed.

"Thomas, you are too funny," Victoria said, chuckling.

"Yeah, Daddy, you should have your own TV show," Keisha added.

"Okay, I want to know what's going on. Y'all never laugh at my jokes. And all this food? How expensive is it? I know somebody bought something."

"Nobody bought anything, you silly man. And why are you being so picky? Can't a woman cook her big, strong man a nice home cooked meal just because?"

"You're right, baby. I shouldn't have jumped to conclusions. I do appreciate it, though. This has been one helluva day."

"You go on and get ready for dinner. I'll set the table."

"Okay, baby," Thomas said, then gave Victoria a peck on the cheek. "And, Keisha, I'm glad to see you're back to your old self again. I was about to go find a priest and have him perform an exorcism on you!"

*****

Thomas showered and later joined the family at dinner. Afterwards, Victoria made a fresh pot of coffee, and they all sat around the table. Keisha led the conversation.

"So, Daddy, how did you like the dinner that Mama prepared for you?"

"Like it? I loved it. Your mama really knows how to throw down in the kitchen," Thomas stated, rubbing his full belly. "Hopefully, you'll be just as good a cook for your husband and family one day, Keisha."

Keisha glimpsed over at Victoria from across the table, looking for sympathy. Victoria returned a wink, coaxing her to get to the point.

Keisha casually addressed Thomas. "Now that you mention it, Daddy, it's funny how you and I think so much alike," she commented, faking a giggle.

Not getting the joke, Thomas wondered why Keisha was laughing. He looked at her strangely.

"Mention what? I didn't say anything," he responded, taking a sip from his cup.

"That thing you said about having a family."

"Yeah, what about it?" Thomas asked, raising a skeptical brow.

Keisha took a big gulp of juice and swallowed.

"Daddy, I have something to tell you, and I'm just going to come right out with it." She stood up and backed away from the table.

"I knew it! I knew it!" Thomas said, shaking his head back and forth. "Y'all take me for a fool, but I'm not as dumb as I look. Well, what is it, Keisha? I wanna know what could be so important that it caused y'all to go through all this trouble for me."

"Daddy, Mommy took me to the emergency room today because I've been feeling sick lately…and I'm pregnant."

Thomas choked on his coffee, spilling the remaining portion in his lap. He jumped up from the table and screamed while fanning his pants. Victoria tried blotting the stains out with a dampened rag, but Thomas grabbed it from her and threw it at the sink counter.

"You're what? How did this happen? I mean, I know how it

happened, but who's the father of the baby?"

"His name is Alvin Williams, Daddy. I've been dating him for a while now," Keisha answered.

Thomas scratched his head. "Alvin Williams...why does that name ring a bell?" He thought for a couple of seconds. "The same Alvin Williams that got arrested with Moe!"

"Yes, sir," Keisha replied.

"What! All those educated young men down at that college you go to, and you settled for that low-life nigga?"

Keisha dropped her head. "I'm sorry, Daddy," she said emotionally.

"Yes, you are sorry, Keisha. I've always had high hopes for you after Jr. turned out the way he did. Now look at you, running 'round here opening your legs to every Tom, Dick, and Harry. You're nothing but a whore. I'm ashamed of you!"

"Thomas!" Victoria yelled in disbelief.

"I call 'em like I see 'em!" he replied.

"That's alright, Mama. He said what he had to say. At least I know the truth now," Keisha cried. "And since you feel that way, Daddy, you ain't ever got to worry about me shaming you no more!"

Keisha ran into her room and returned with two packed suitcases, carrying them to the front door.

"Do you see what you've done, Thomas? Our daughter is leaving!" Victoria shouted.

"Well, if that's what she wants, then let her go. Ain't nobody stopping her." He looked at Keisha. "I'll tell you what, though. If you walk out that door, don't come back!"

"He didn't mean it, Keisha. Thomas, tell her you didn't mean it," Victoria pleaded.

"I will not!" Thomas answered stubbornly.

"Don't beg him, Mama. I can't stay another minute in this house with that man anyway. I'm outta here!" Keisha said and slammed the door behind her.

Halfway up the block, Keisha turned into Cece's yard. When she got on the front porch, she sat the suitcases down and banged on the door.

Cece came down, toting Jahlil on her hip.

"Keisha, why the hell are you banging on my door like you the police? And what's with the bags? You going somewhere?"

Keisha broke down crying. "I had to get away from that crazy-ass man, Cece. You should have heard what he said to me. He called me out of my name and everything," she said, bawling.

"Calm down, girl. I can't understand a word you're saying," Cece said. "Grab your stuff and come upstairs."

"Thanks," Keisha said, following Cece.

When they got upstairs, Cece sat Jahlil in his walker and gave him a squeeze toy to play with. She had Keisha put her bags in the hall closet. She gave her a box of Kleenex tissues to wipe her tears, and then they went into Cece's bedroom.

"Now from the beginning, tell me what happened over there that got you acting all hysterical. And don't leave anything out."

Keisha wiped her eyes and blew her nose. "What didn't happen?" she said. "It was like World War II in that house. Everything that could possibly go wrong did. My mother took me down to the hospital today. I'm pregnant, Cece."

Cece was dumbfounded. "Get the fuck outta here, Keisha. For real?" she asked.

"Yes, for real, Cece," Keisha assured her. "Why else would I be here with two suitcases?"

"Oh shit! So they threw you out?" Cece asked, giggling. "And sorry, I ain't mean to laugh at you."

"No, they didn't throw me out. I left. You know my father was hot, though. He called me a whore and everything else in the book."

"Ooh, Keisha, no he didn't," Cece said. "I've seen you and

your pops duke it out before, but I've never heard him cuss."

"Shit, you should have heard him, Cece. When I told him about the baby, he just changed all of a sudden. It's like he had a split personality. You know, like Dr. Jekyll and Mr. Hyde."

"Damn, I missed out. So you just up and left, huh?"

"Yeah, basically, but I'm going to need a place to stay. Do you think your mom will let me crash here until I can get on my feet?" Keisha asked.

"It shouldn't be a problem. You know that's your second mother, and you practically lived here before you hooked up with what's his face. It is his baby, right?" Cece asked.

"His name ain't no damn what's his face; it's Detroit," Keisha clarified. "And what you mean is it his? Who else have I slept with?"

"You tell me. You're the one pregnant," Cece said. "But, what are you going to do about cash? You lost your job laying up in the bed like a zombie."

"I know. That was dumb," Keisha admitted.

"No man ain't worth crying over, Keisha. Believe me, I know from experience. You think I sat around here moping and shit when I got pregnant with Jahlil? My mama wasn't even having it. I worked right up until my last trimester, and she ain't gonna let you sit around this house either. You better start looking through them want ads in the paper."

"I know that, Cece. I'll find another job somewhere."

"But, until then, you still gotta eat," Cece said. "In the morning, I'm taking you down to welfare to get emergency food stamps."

"What kinda shit you on? I ain't begging nobody for no damn food stamps," Keisha declared.

"You might as well come down off that high horse and swallow your pride," Cece insisted. "How do you think I get by? And you ain't got shit anyway, so beggars can't be choosey."

"I guess you're right. It'll have to do for now," Keisha agreed. "Because I'm not going back to that house. You can bet money on that."

"I hear you," Cece responded. "Now get some rest. Tomorrow's a big day."

*****

Keisha and Cece got up early the next morning and took the city bus down to the Department of Social Services. On the way out, Keisha saw Thomas leaving for work, but neither of them spoke a word to the other.

When they got inside the welfare office, Keisha took a number at the service desk and waited to be seen. The waiting room was crowded and the atmosphere depressing. It seemed like there were more people inside the building looking for assistance than the actual number of people that had jobs on the outside. Keisha and Cece passed the time by doing crossword puzzles and reading outdated magazines from the display shelf. There was also enough animated personalities in the facility to keep them entertained, so there was never a dull moment.

It was two hours before someone called Keisha to the back. When the interview was done, she sat and waited to see another caseworker, who asked her for more personal information and made her fill out more paperwork. The cycle repeated until Keisha ended up spending half of the day downtown. On a positive note, she was prepared for each interview. Cece gave Keisha the rundown on how the system worked and quizzed her on what and what not to say. The most important thing Keisha had to remember was to report that the baby's father had abandoned her, and that she didn't know of his whereabouts. Sadly, in Keisha's case, this was true because Detroit had no knowledge of her pregnancy.

Three months passed before Keisha was accepted for public

assistance. She celebrated like she had won the state lottery when she received the award letter and three hundred dollars in food stamps. The following month, she moved into her first apartment. It was a cheap, rundown, shabby tenement that she found on Warrick Street, but it was all she could afford. There was no better feeling than having a place of her own. Keisha appreciated Cece and her mother for putting her up for so long, but she couldn't wait to get away from them. Clara was always pestering Keisha about getting a job, even though she accepted whatever day's work they gave her at the employment agency.

Cece stopped tending to Jahlil altogether. It was Keisha that got up at night whenever Jahlil hollered for a bottle or needed another diaper change. Keisha even became the designated babysitter when Cece went out on dates. So, it was odd that Keisha permitted her request to move in after Clara put her out for inviting her boyfriends to sleep over.

Keisha and Thomas still weren't talking, but she did keep in touch with Victoria on a daily basis. They phoned each other and talked for hours until it was time for Thomas to come home. On certain days, Keisha would stop by the house while Thomas was at the barbershop and pick Victoria up so they could go shopping for the baby and have lunch. Keisha always saw to it that her mother arrived home safely, but she never stepped foot in the door. It hurt Victoria that Thomas and Keisha had distanced themselves from each other, but she hoped their differences would be put aside once the baby was born.

In June of 1976, Keisha Johnson became the proud mother of a newborn son. She named him Foster, which was Thomas's middle name. Thomas didn't acknowledge his grandson until Victoria told him that the baby resembled him. Honestly, Foster looked exactly like his father, so Detroit could never deny his son if he ever saw him. However, Thomas always asked about Keisha during the pregnancy and sent her money by Victoria from time to time.

Keisha continued with her classes until the end of her second trimester with the baby. She stopped going after back pains persisted. She had planned on returning to college, but it was hard finding a babysitter that she felt comfortable with. Victoria volunteered to watch the baby, but that wouldn't work. Keisha knew Thomas would only hold it over her head once they had a fallout, and she was one step ahead of him.

Cece moved out and got an apartment in the same building after Keisha stopped watching Jahlil for her, but they remained the best of friends. Cece recommended her babysitter to Keisha, but she refused the offer. It would have been convenient for Keisha to use the young woman because she lived in the neighborhood. However, she already had three kids of her own, and she wasn't even taking care of them properly.

Chapter 14

Sonny Blake

A year later, Keisha attended a neighborhood block party, where she met Sonny Blake. Keisha was skeptical about dating again at first. She had turned down quite a few offers from some of Brooklyn's most eligible bachelors. Partly because there was some shred of hope that Detroit would return. But, that never happened, so she moved on.

Unlike Detroit, who had business savvy, Sonny grew up in the streets and had a street mentality. His mother was a heroin addict, and she relied on prostitution to support her habit. Taken from his mother at the age of ten, Sonny became a property of the state. He lived with different families in the foster care system and often ran away.

By the time he reached puberty, Sonny was sent to a maximum-security juvenile facility, and he resided in such places until he escaped at age sixteen. Once Sonny was free, he became a member of an organized street gang and began on a bizarre reign of crimes throughout the city, which eventually landed him in jail.

Sonny served a one-year sentence in Riker's Island state prison for burglarizing a jewelry store, and was out on parole for good behavior when he met Keisha. So, the timing was perfect. Upon the terms of his release, Sonny needed a permanent address and a job.

Having a knack for fixing cars, he found employment at an auto body repair shop on Stone Avenue. He used a friend's house temporarily for visits from his P.O., but time was running out. That's where Keisha fit in.

Sonny swept Keisha off her feet with his charm and the ripped, bronzed, muscular physique that he acquired while incarcerated. He was also a smooth talker, so it didn't take long for Keisha to fall for the bait. Within the third week of their relationship, Sonny had persuaded Keisha to let him move in with her.

Keisha was glad to have a man around the house again. Her brother T.J. stayed with her temporarily after Cece moved out. However, he was always stealing from her, so she had to put him out. Sonny had other plans for T.J., but he would have to put them on hold until the timing was right.

The following year, Keisha gave birth to her second son, Malik. Malik had Sonny's medium brown complexion, but he favored his mother Keisha otherwise. Keisha had a new man in her life, and she was happy again. Sonny was a good father to his son, and he treated Foster as his own from the beginning.

Another two years went by, and Sonny's parole probation was complete. Sonny kept his job at the body shop, but along with his new freedom came a new change of pattern in his lifestyle. He no longer had a curfew to come home straight after work, and he often didn't. Sonny also reacquainted himself with old habits and spent hours on end catching up on old times. Before long, Cece and T.J. joined in, and it was one big happy family.

Chapter 15

Rise and Shine

Sonny awoke from his sleep at 9:30 a.m. Realizing that Keisha wasn't in bed, he called out for her. When she didn't answer, he got up to see what was going on. It took Sonny a minute to get to his feet because he was hungover. The card game lasted until four o'clock in the morning, and they had to put people out in order to end it.

Sonny made his way to the bathroom and relieved himself, then brushed his teeth. When he saw that Keisha wasn't in the living room, he checked to see if the boys were up, but they were sound asleep. He cursed Cece under his breath when he saw she had managed to leave again without taking Jahlil with her. Upon reaching the kitchen, he stood in the doorway to find Keisha sitting at the kitchen table in a daze. Keisha didn't notice Sonny approaching her.

"Good morning," he said, giving her a peck on the cheek.

"Ooh, you scared the shit out of me, Sonny. I told you about sneaking up on me!" Keisha said as she jumped.

"Shit, you were in a trance. I stood at the door for at least five minutes watching you before I came in. What you in here thinking so hard about?"

"Nothing much. Just daydreaming, I guess," she answered.

"If you call that daydreaming, then you need to take your ass back to bed," Sonny said humorously. "You were so out of it that the house could have caught on fire, and you wouldn't have known until you got burnt!"

"Whatever," Keisha replied, dumping her cigarette in the ashtray. "Let me get up so I can start breakfast for my babies. You should be hungry, too. You hardly ate a thing last night."

"I can't eat when I'm playing cards, baby. I gotta stay focused."

"How can you stay focused if you're high all the time, Sonny?" Keisha asked. "You blacked out before everyone left, and I had to help you get into bed. What you need to do is cut down on that shit."

"No. What you need to do is get me an Alka Seltzer and shut the fuck up! I done told you to stop trying to change me, Keisha. I don't know how your last man got down, but I'm grown. You can't tell me shit!"

"And who the fuck do you think you're talking to? You must have me confused with the last bitch you was fucking. I'm trying to talk some sense into your sorry ass. Then to make matters worse, you got my brother and my best friend hooked, too. I told you that I didn't want you bringing that shit into my house any damn way!" Keisha yelled.

"Oh, so now this is your house, and I don't do shit, right? That's what you trying to say, Keisha?"

"Well, it must be mine, because I don't see your name nowhere on my lease!" she remarked.

Sonny's eyes turned blood red. He was already hot, and Keisha's remark only added fuel to the fire. She was at the sink rinsing dishes off, when Sonny rushed at Keisha, snatched her by the arm, and spun her around. He raised his free hand to slap Keisha across the face, but caught himself when he felt the sharp edge of the butcher knife that she held at his throat.

"I wish you would, motherfucker!" she said.

Sonny got the shock of his life. He straightened up and put on a smile.

"Damn, baby, what's up with all the violence? Can't you take a joke? I wasn't really gonna hit you," he said, trying to lie his way out of a rock and a hard place.

"I hope not, because I will use this, if I have to," she told him, waving the knife.

"That's my baby. She ain't scared of nobody, not even me." Sonny gave Keisha a quick peck on the lips. "You weren't really gonna cut me, were you, baby?" he asked.

"I guess we'll never know, now will we?" Keisha said, kissing him back. "Just don't get any more ideas about putting your hands on me."

"I feel you on that, mama," Sonny said, while playfully groping Keisha's behind. "Let me go wake them three knuckleheads up before you get me started." He walked to the doorway and turned back. "Keisha, that damn Cece done dipped on us again and left Jahlil. Why do you keep letting her get over like that? I wouldn't mind if she wasn't so sneaky about it."

"It wasn't even like that this time, baby," Keisha answered. "That girl got so high, she went out in the hall and peed behind the stairwell. Then, she cussed Melvin out and tried to fight him. I had to take her ass home. Jahlil was already here, so I let him sleep with the boys. She wasn't in any condition to look after him no how."

"We did have a good time last night, didn't we, baby?"

"It was cool until all that dumb shit started," Keisha commented. "But, we're going to have to start closing it up a little earlier from now on. I'm not having people disrespecting my house every week. If that's the case, I'll stop everybody from coming in here. I got a few words for Cece's ass, too, when I see her again."

"Whatchu mean, when you see her again? She better come down here to get her son!"

"Oh, she will. I'll let her sleep another hour or two. Then I'll give her a call," Keisha told him. "Now, go and wake the boys for me...please."

"Alright, baby, I got you," Sonny said and left the kitchen.

Chapter 16

Do I Get a Pass?

Sonny returned carrying Malik in his arm, with Jahlil and Foster trotting behind. He handed Keisha the baby and left the room again. Keisha sat Malik in his highchair and seated the boys at the table. She grabbed a huge bag of generic wheat puffs from the top of the fridge. It was so heavy that it took both hands to pour it into the bowls. She added sugar and milk, and told the boys to say their grace. They put their hands together and sang.

> *God our Father*
> *God our Father*
> *Once again*
> *Thank you for our blessings*
> *Thank you for our blessings*
> *Amen*
> *Amen.*

Keisha hand-fed Malik as he devoured every morsel of food that entered his little mouth. She looked over at Jahlil and Foster to find them both staring at the bowls.

"What's going on over there?" she asked. "Neither of you have touched your cereal."

"Auntie, are you gonna get mad at me if I say something?" Jahlil asked.

Here this boy goes again, Keisha thought. "No, Jahlil, I won't get mad," she said. "But, you better not say anything smart. I done warned you about that fresh mouth of yours."

"It ain't bad, Auntie. It's about this," he said, pointing to the cereal.

"Okay, Jahlil, what is it?"

"Why do I gotta eat the cereal from the cheap aisle every time I come here? Ain't y'all got money?"

Keisha's face lit up. "What are you talking about, little boy? That cereal came from the same aisle as the other boxes in the store. There's nothing wrong with it. It's just like the Sugar Bear cereal; they just make it at a different company."

"But, Auntie, this ain't a box. It's a bag. Look, you can see through it," Jahlil said, pressing his face closely against the package. "And it taste nasty," he added.

"Well, it shouldn't, Jahlil. I put enough sugar in y'all bowls for you to taste it."

Foster raised his hand. "Mommy, I know what he's talking about," he said.

"Oh Lord, not you, too!" Keisha said, feeling as if a gang of midgets was attacking her. "What is he talking about, Foster?"

"Mommy, do I get a pass to say it?" he asked.

"Do you get a pass to say what, Foster?" Sonny stepped into the kitchen. He was headed to the corner store to buy a blunt, when he heard the boys complaining. Foster got scared and closed his mouth.

"I wanna hear this," Sonny said. "Go ahead and speak your mind, little man. You get the pass."

"Are you sure, Sonny?"

"Boy, I done gave you the pass. Stop being so scary."

Foster looked around the room. After building up enough

95

courage, he said, "It tastes like shit!"

Everyone burst out laughing, including the baby, who thought they were playing a game.

"You are something else, boy," Sonny said. "Look, I'm going to the store. Who wants a box of Frank N' Berries?"

"Yay!" they all screamed, jumping up and down.

*****

Sonny met Cece in the hall. She was half drunk and came out of her apartment wearing a short thin robe that barely came past her waistline, and it was loose at the belt. All she wore underneath were her panties, and her breasts were exposed. Cece walked past Sonny, bumping him on the shoulder. She then turned around angrily and confronted him.

"Hey, motherfucker, what's your problem? You better watch where the fuck you going. Next time, I'm gonna cut your ass!"

"Cece, wake your drunk ass up. It's me…Sonny."

Cece squinted through half-closed eyes. When she realized it was Sonny, she broke out in a big laugh.

"Oh shit, it's the baddest nigga on the planet. Everybody take cover because Sonny Blake is in the motherfucking building!" she cracked. "What you know good, Sonny?"

"Not a damn thing, you drunk ass. And what the hell is wrong with you coming out here like that? Your titties are showing!"

"What, you ain't never seen none of these before?" she asked, swinging the house robe open, exposing her breast in full view. Sonny checked Cece out for a minute. She was appealing, but when he came to his senses, he grabbed Cece and covered her up.

"Are you out of your fucking mind?" he yelled as he tied her belt. "What if someone were to walk by and see this shit? They might get the wrong idea!"

"Ain't nobody gonna think shit, Sonny. Stop being so

paranoid."

"Are you on your way to my house? 'Cause if you are, you need to get going."

"Yeah, I'm going. You don't have to tell me twice," Cece said. Sonny started towards the back exit, but Cece stopped him. "Hey, where are you going?"

"I'm not going any further than the corner to get a blunt, so don't ask me to bring nothing back," Sonny replied.

"See...I wasn't gonna ask you to bring nothing, for your information."

"So what you call me for then?" Sonny asked.

"Are you sharing that blunt when you get back? I need to get lit."

"That's a damn shame, Cece. You still high from last night, and you talking about getting lit? You ain't asked a thing about your son or nothing."

"I am concerned about my son, and you need to mind your own business."

"If you're so concerned, then why am I going to buy your son breakfast?"

"You must be buying it for your own kids, because I got food in the house for my child. I take good care of mine!"

"If you were taking care of him, he wouldn't be at my house, Cece. You pull the same shit every weekend. You come through with Jahlil, and the next thing I know, you at the club, and we're stuck with him. You need to stay your ass at home and be a mother to that boy. He already ain't got no daddy."

"How can you preach to me about staying home when you're always in the streets your damn self? Keisha don't know where you are half the time, and ain't no telling what you be doing. But, don't worry about my son sleeping at your house again, because when I take him home, he ain't never going back there!" Cece said, then stormed down the hall.

"Is that a threat, Cece? Because if so, I can live with it," Sonny said.

"Fuck you, Sonny!" Cece shot back, sticking her middle finger up. When she got to the door, Keisha was waiting on her.

"Cece, who are you arguing with now? Me and the kids heard you from the kitchen. And what do you have on?" she asked.

"It's a house robe, Keisha, just like the one you got on; because I was in the house!" she exaggerated. "Now are you gonna keep blocking the door or are you gonna let me in?"

"Come on inside, drunky," Keisha replied.

When Cece walked in and sat at the table with the kids, one of her breasts popped out of the house robe. Foster flashed a boyish grin.

"Why are you staring at me, little man, and whatchu smiling about?" Cece asked.

Foster held his head down bashfully and giggled. Cece knew what was going on after that.

"Oh, you like these, huh?" she asked him.

Foster turned his head and covered his eyes.

"Cece, cover your titties, girl!" Keisha yelled. "Don't be coming in here flashing your goodies in front of my babies. They're too young for that!"

"Damn, Keisha, it's only flesh. What's the big deal? I get dressed in front of Jahlil all the time."

"Well, I don't do that in front of my boys, not with Foster anyway. So, I'd appreciate it if you kept those things covered up." Keisha went into her bedroom and returned with a pair of gym shorts and a t-shirt for Cece. "Here, go in the bathroom and put these on. Sonny's coming back soon, and he don't need to be seeing your stuff either."

"Alright, Keisha, damn." Cece replied, then went into the bathroom, and slipped into the clothes. "Whatchu cooking for breakfast?" she asked when she came out.

"I'm not cooking this morning. Sonny just went out to get the kids a box of cereal," Keisha told her. "Your son didn't approve of what I gave him earlier. He asked me why I bought the cheap brand."

"What did I tell you about being disrespectful, boy?" Cece screamed at Jahlil. "I'ma beat ya ass when we get home. Now, apologize to Auntie Keisha."

"I'm sorry, Auntie Keisha," Jahlil said, now crying.

"It's alright, baby," Keisha replied. "But wait, Cece, it wasn't just Jahlil. His running buddy told me the cereal tastes like shit," she said, pointing to Foster.

"Keisha, you should have knocked the mess out of both of them."

"I was about to, but it was so funny that I had to laugh myself. You had to be here."

"It probably was funny, but Jahlil knows I don't play that shit," Cece answered while lighting a cigarette.

"Wait a minute. You still haven't told me who you were fussing with out there," Keisha said.

"Girl, my head's so fucked up I don't even remember," Cece admitted. "It could have been the mailman for all I know."

"That's a shame, Cece," Keisha said.

Just then, Sonny walked in the door and gave Cece a dirty look.

"Oh, the lush is still here," he said, setting a bag on the table. "I thought you'd be gone by the time I got back."

"What is he talking about, Cece?" Keisha asked.

"Hell if I know. I haven't seen him since last night."

"Last night? I just spoke to you a few minutes ago, Cece. Don't you remember?" Sonny asked.

"I swear I don't, but I'll take your word for it," she replied.

"Damn, Cece, you're that tore up? Let me go fix you a hot cup of coffee," Keisha said.

"Thank you, girl. I'd appreciate it."

While heading towards the bedroom, Sonny said, "I'll leave you two alone to gossip."

Keisha followed him, closing the door behind them. "Hey, did you and Cece get into an argument? I heard her fussing with somebody."

"Nah, baby. We had a few words, but nothing major," Sonny answered.

He wasn't about to bring up the argument and start a new one, so he left it alone.

Chapter 17

Making Ends Meet

Keisha was barely getting by on the bi-weekly check that she received from public assistance. There were even times when she couldn't rub two dimes together. The rent was always overdue, and when it was paid, there was hardly any money left over. The food stamps did help out to an extent, but with the rise of the economy, groceries never lasted throughout the month. To make matters worse, Sonny got fired from his job at the auto body shop. The owner told him that the business was downsizing, but he really needed the spot to hire his son-in-law. Sonny went from one job interview to the next, trying to find work so he could support his family, but he would get the same feedback wherever he went. It was always, "We don't have any openings at the moment," even though there were Help Wanted signs in the windows when he got there. Or the usual, "We'll give you a call" pitch, but no one ever called back. Sonny wasn't dumb. He knew no one would hire an ex-con with a criminal record. He would have to step his game up.

The lack of money often brought on conflict between Keisha and Sonny. They became distant, except for when they argued, which was almost every day, and there was never any peace in the household. It affected the kids, as well. They often went to bed hungry because there was no food in the house. One night when

Sonny came home, he and Keisha had a dispute over their living conditions.

"So did you find anything today?" Keisha asked.

"Damn, Keisha, I barely set foot in the door, and you starting already," Sonny complained. "Don't I even get a 'hello' or 'how was your day' first?"

"I'm sorry, baby. You're right," Keisha said. She walked up to Sonny, threw her arms around his neck, and gave him a kiss. "Hi, baby. How was your day?"

"Now that's more like it. That's how a woman's supposed to greet her man," Sonny replied and slapped Keisha on the butt. He then opened a can of beer that he had brought home.

"Oh, we're celebrating, are we? It must have been a good day."

"I don't consider drinking a beer as celebrating, if that's what you mean. I just needed to have one. But, I did make a couple of dollars shooting craps. Here you go." Sonny threw fifty dollars on the kitchen table.

After counting the money out, she threw it back at him.

"What is this, Sonny? We've got bills to pay. This ain't even enough to bargain with. And how did you find the time to shoot craps, when you were supposed to be out there looking for a job?"

"I did look for a job, Keisha. There just ain't nothing out there for me."

"Well, you better do something. We can't continue to live like this. You know I only get so much from welfare. We need more money coming in the house."

"Keisha, I'm doing what I can," Sonny said. "Can't you go down to the welfare office and let them folks know that you need more? At least until I can figure something out."

"That's a good idea. How much more do you think I should ask for? Maybe a hundred thousand? Or better yet, let's go for broke. I'll just go down there and demand they give me a million dollars. That'll show them!"

"See, why you gotta be a smart ass, Keisha? It was only a suggestion," he said.

"And it was a stupid one, Sonny. How do you expect me to go ask them white folks for more money, when they don't want to give it in the first place?" Keisha asked. "It's bad enough that I have to beg them for what I'm getting now. You should see the looks on their faces when I'm trying to explain how I got pregnant and don't know where the baby's daddy is. You don't know what I have to go through, Sonny. It's humiliating."

Sonny took a swig of the beer. "Damn, baby, I didn't know it was that rough, but don't you worry none. I'll just have to hustle a little harder, that's all. We'll be alright."

"Hustling ain't gonna get it, Sonny. You need to find a stable job. We're a month behind in the rent, and the landlord keeps harassing me. If we don't come up with the money soon, he's going to put us out on the street. I've been looking in the want ads myself. I saw a couple of possibilities."

Sonny beat his fist on the table. "No way! You need to be at home with the boys. And besides, I support for my own!"

"Not with this chump change," Keisha said, referring to the crap money. "Have you been listening to me? We are ass out!" she said, starting to cry.

Sonny pulled Keisha to his lap and gave her a comforting hug. "Look, baby, I'm going to be honest with you," he said. "Nobody out there is trying to hire me with my record. It just ain't gonna happen. But like I said, I don't want you in here worrying about nothing. Things are gonna look up for us real soon. I've got a big score in the works."

"What are you going to do, Sonny? I hope it isn't illegal."

"Look, baby, you just said yourself that we needed the money. And are you forgetting about the boys? They're growing faster by the minute. They need clothes, shoes, and everything else in between. If this job pays off like I think it will, we'll be straight."

"That's all good, Sonny, but I don't want you getting into any trouble. And I definitely don't want you to get hurt."

"That's just a chance I'll have to take, baby," Sonny replied. "Nothing in this world worth having comes easy. But, why are you talking so negative, woman? Don't you have any faith in me?"

"You know I do. Just be safe. I don't know what I would do if something were to happen to you."

"Ain't shit gonna happen to me, baby. I need you to be strong right now, Keisha. You're my good luck charm. Now tell me that you trust me."

Now where have I heard that before? Keisha thought. "I trust you, baby," she said.

Chapter 18

Desperados

The game plan was in progress, but time was ticking. The strategy was pretty basic. Go into the East New York Savings Bank, rob it blind, and be out. It was as simple as that; nothing more or less. Of course, there were still a few minor details that had to be sorted out.

For one, Sonny had to put together a crew that he felt was confident enough to pull the job off, and they had to be trustworthy. With little time on his hands, Sonny brought in Keisha's brother, T.J., who was a petty thief and stole for nickels and dimes. Still, he had just enough heart to get the job done. Then there was Pablo Vega, a Puerto Rican cat with slicked hair and tattoos all over his body. He had been Sonny's cellmate back in Riker's and looked out for him when he first got there. Vega only stood at five-eight, but he got the most respect when he was on the block. He got sent up on a murder rap for killing a guy in front of a liquor store who was just looking at his girlfriend. The charges were dropped to involuntary manslaughter when no witnesses appeared on the day of his court hearing.

Vega's cousin, Antonio, was one of the best gun suppliers in the game, so that put a checkmark on the necessary firearms needed for the job.

Next was securing a getaway car and a driver. When Sonny worked at the repair shop, he was given a spare key that opened the gate to the lot. Sonny had made a copy for himself, which was still in his possession. On Saturday nights, he would go back to the shop after closing, take one of the fixed vehicles for a joyride; and have it back early Sunday morning. The keys were always left in the ignition of the cars because the lot was well guarded by two full-grown Doberman Pinschers, Zulu and King. The dogs knew Sonny, so it was no problem getting past them.

Sonny and Vega stole a white '74 dodge van the night before and parked it in Vega's garage overnight for safekeeping. Last but not least, Cece was chosen as the designated driver for the initial getaway.

The crew met up at Vega's house on Friday at 7:30 a.m. as planned. The bank opened at nine o'clock, which gave them a little over an hour's time to plan before the big score. As they stood around a wooden worktable in the garage, Vega unloaded the artillery and a duffle bag filled with masks, gloves, and other accessories. While he distributed a set to each man, Sonny removed a hand drawn map from his pocket.

"Okay, everybody, listen up and pay close attention," he said, unfolding the map and spreading it on the table. "We must have gone over this a hundred times, so everyone should know their positions by now. But, just to make sure no one was sleeping in class, we'll do a last-minute check.

"Cece will go into the bank, walk up to the teller's window, and open an account. Eventually, someone will come out and escort her here." He pointed at a desk area drawn on the map. "T.J. will be stationed here at the diner across the street, waiting for Cece's signal. When he gets it, he'll come over and distract the security guard. Vega and I will be parked here." He pointed to the map again. "We'll pull the car up and rush the door. Cece will come out and take the wheel. From there, we grab the money and be out within five minutes. That should be enough time to get the job done before some lucky bastard sets the alarm." Sonny removed a cigarette from his pocket, lit it, and took a long drag. "Are there any questions?" he asked.

"None from me. I'm ready to do this," Vega said, waving a semi-automatic .45 with a coldhearted snarl on his face.

"That's my nigga Vega. Always ready to go to war," Sonny commented with a cocky smile.

"You know it," Vega replied.

"I feel you, but remember, this is a clean job," Sonny told him. "Don't run up in there like the mercenaries blowing shit up. Let's keep it nice and clean."

Vega put the gun away. "Relax, holmes. I'm cool."

T.J. raised his hand. "Hey, I have a question. What am I supposed to do to keep myself busy? I mean, I'll be sitting right at the counter. What if a waitress comes by?"

Sonny looked at T.J. and thought, *This has got to be the most simple-minded negro on the whole planet.*

"Are you for real?" Sonny asked. "There are a million other things that could go wrong, and you're worried about a fucking waitress?"

"You never know," T.J. replied, shrugging his shoulders.

Vega jumped in. "Sonny, where did you find this puta? This is a waste of time."

T.J. didn't know what "puta" meant, but he knew he had been insulted. He looked around the room. "Yo, what did this fried green banana-eating motherfucker just call me?"

Vega simply grinned.

A short, stubby woman with a noticeable mustache opened the door that adjoined the house to the garage. It was Vega's mother.

"Pablo, what is going on down there?" she yelled, standing with her hands on her hips.

Vega met her at the foot of the stairs. "Mami, this is not the right time. Go back inside."

After Vega's mom uttered a few words in Spanish and left, Vega returned to the group.

"Hey, puta, lower your voice," he told T.J.

Sonny started getting pissed. "Would you two please cut the bullshit!" he snarled through tightly clenched teeth. "If it's that important to you, T.J., then order a coffee. Hell, you can order the whole fucking menu for all I care. Just be ready."

"I'll be ready," T.J. said, taking his gun.

Cece looks at everyone in the garage. She was the only one who didn't have a weapon, so she addressed Sonny.

"Hold on. Why is everybody strapped except me? I know y'all don't think I'm finna roll without a gat."

"That's a good point, Cece. It's better to be safe than sorry," Sonny responded. "Vega, you got anything that Cece can hold?"

"Why should she have a gun? There's no danger involved in her part. I told you I didn't feel comfortable working with no bitches anyway!" Vega barked.

"Who the fuck is you calling a bitch, esé? Your mama's a bitch!" Cece fired back.

"Yo, Sonny, you need to check your girl," Vega warned.

"Sonny don't need to do a muthafuckin' thing. This is between me and you. So, come get some if you want some!" Cece dared.

"Maybe later, mami," Vega replied, then wagged his tongue in a sexual manner.

"Fuck you, Chico!" Cece shot back.

Sonny whistled through his fingers. It eased the bickering, but there was still tension in the room. "Will you two get it together! We can't do this shit effectively unless we act as a team. I'm not about to risk my fucking life over a lover's quarrel. We've just wasted an hour, and it's thirty minutes until show time. Do you think you can behave until then?"

"Hey, I'm in it to win it," Vega responded. "You should be

asking her."

"You know I'm wit' it, Sonny," Cece added, then turned to Vega. "I'll get back to your ass later," she said with a vindictive stare.

"I'll be waiting for you," Vega confirmed.

"That's what I wanted to hear," Sonny said, breaking the controversy. "Now how about that other piece, Vega?"

"Oh yeah, I've got something just for her, but it's upstairs. Give me a sec." Vega went into the house and returned with a .22. "Here you go, mami," he said, handing it to Cece.

Cece frowned as she took it from him. "What is this, a fucking cap gun?" she asked.

"Hey, that's all I got. Take it or leave it. And I want it back, too!" Vega replied.

"Oh, don't worry. You're gonna get yours!" Cece promised.

*****

It was 8:55 a.m., and traffic pushed along the streets as pedestrians combed the pavement of their morning route in opposite paths. Inside the East New York Savings Bank on Atlantic Avenue, the vault had been opened by the bank manager, a middle-aged man who was now sitting behind his desk browsing through reports. A dumpy-looking security guard, whose gut hung over his belt, unhooked the velvet rope barrier at the front door and flipped the light switch on. Three tellers sat behind sectioned windows and had just set up their money drawers. They patiently awaited the crowd that was standing outside.

Sonny was parked on the corner of Pennsylvania Avenue, parallel to the bank's location. He kept a watchful eye. The guard unlocked the door at 9:00 a.m. sharp, and fifteen or so civilians rushed in. Watching from behind the tinted windshield inside the van, Sonny alerted the team.

"Okay, it's showtime," he told them.

Cece and T.J. jumped out. Cece was disguised in a wig, mirrored sunglasses, and dressed in a two-piece skirt outfit with a matching purse. She primped herself and then walked confidently into the bank. T.J., who was clad in an Afro wig and dark shades, hit Sonny up for five dollars and headed to the diner.

As Cece approached the bank's entrance, the security guard opened the door for her. She thanked him, and he returned a friendly smile. He snuck a glimpse of her plump derrière once she walked past him and shook his head in admiration. The civilians formed lines and began their transactions with the tellers. Cece stepped into one of the lines as five more people entered the building. She waited as the line slowly moved forward. Finally, a blonde-haired woman with a blank expression called out, "Next!"

Cece approached the window.

"Good morning. How may I help you?" she asked without much enthusiasm.

Cece put on a smile. "Good morning. I'd like to open an account, please."

"What type of account are you requesting to open?"

"A checking account," Cece responded.

The teller handed Cece a clipboard and some brochures.

"Please move from the line and fill this out. You can return it to any one of the tellers when you're done. Next!" she called out, looking past Cece.

Cece snatched the clipboard from the teller's hand and walked to a counter along the wall. *I won't be going back to that snotty bitch,* she thought. After completing the application form, she returned to the window and handed it to a woman with a more cheerful attitude.

"Thank you," the teller said, taking the clipboard. "One of our representatives will be with you shortly."

Moments later, an elegant-looking woman appeared. The

nametag on her blouse read *Doris Livingston.*

"Crystal Howard!" she called out, which was the name Cece had written on the application. Cece stalled until she remembered that she was Crystal Howard. She raised her hand and then followed the woman to a desk, where they both took a seat.

"Hello, Ms. Howard. I'm Doris Livingston. I'll be your representative for the day. How may I help you?"

Again with the questions. I just told the other bitch, Cece thought to herself. She forced another smile and replied, "I'd like to open a checking account, please."

"Okay, and how much would you like to start the account with?"

"What's the minimal requirement?" Cece asked.

"That would be a standard account; twenty dollars," Doris responded.

Cece reached into her purse, and opened the zippered compartment. "Perfect, 'cause that's all I got."

"Fine. I will need a copy of your driver's license first, and then we can get you started."

That was Cece's cue. She covered her mouth with her hand and began to fake a cough.

"Is there something wrong?" Doris asked.

"It's my allergies. Must be something in the air," Cece said. "Could I trouble you for a glass of water?"

Doris stood up. "Why, of course, Ms. Howard. It would be my pleasure."

As she walked away, Cece flashed the window blinds. That was T.J.'s cue to give the thumbs-up on his end, but he did not respond.

Doris returned with the water. "Here you go, Ms. Howard," she said, handing Cece the water. "I hope this helps."

Cece took the glass from Doris. There still was no sign from T.J. After drinking the water, she politely handed the empty glass to Doris.

"Do you think I could have another one? I'm still a little parched."

Doris wasn't thrilled about having to run back and forth, but she obliged. "Sure, Ms. Howard."

Cece flashed the blinds again, but nothing happened. Then she parted them barely enough to peek through, and there was T.J. sitting at the counter, spreading jelly on some type of bread.

Cece was infuriated. "Look at this fool eating a damn bagel. He better turn his fucking head towards this window," she whispered under her breath.

She flashed the blinds once more. This time, T.J. noticed and started choking on his beverage, but finally returned the signal.

Doris came back with the empty glass and a full pitcher of ice water.

"Now this should hold you for a while," she said.

*****

After paying the tab, T.J. left the diner. As he stepped off the curb, a squad car with two officers probing the vicinity passed by. His heart started to beat faster with fear as he stepped back on the curb. After the close call, he dashed across the street and entered the bank.

Sonny and Vega saw him go inside. They pulled off the main street and swung into the parking lot of the bank.

The guard opened the door for T.J.

"Good morning," he said.

"Good morning, sir," T.J. replied. "Excuse me, but can you direct me to the restroom? It's an emergency."

"Sure, it's right this way," the guard responded.

As he led the way, T.J. removed the .45 from his jacket and butted him on the back of the head. The stunned security guard fell

113

to his knees and reached for the .38 in his holster, but T.J. kicked him in the jaw. Several of his teeth flew across the room with a stream of bloody spit. As T.J. took the guard's gun, Sonny and Vega stormed through the door with their guns extended at arm's length. Sonny carried a black briefcase, and both men wore masks and black gloves.

Vega locked the door, and Sonny fired a shot through the ceiling to get everyone's attention.

"Everybody on the floor, facedown!" he yelled.

The frightened civilians screamed, but they obeyed.

Vega spotted the nameplate on the bank manager's desk as he got up.

"Stay where you are," he ordered him.

Vega looked up. There was a security monitor above the bank manager's desk. He blasted at the screen, which shattered into tiny pieces. The horrified bank manager covered his head and curled into a fetal position. T.J. hurried to the teller's window while Vega covered the door.

In the meantime, Doris, the representative, reached to activate the alarm that was located on the side of the desk. However, Cece went into her purse, pulled out the .22, and stuck it in Doris's face.

"I wouldn't do that if I were you!" she told her. Then she walked Doris to the center of the bank and pushed her to the floor. She went to the side exit, but the door was locked.

"I can't get out!" she yelled.

Vega snatched the keys from the belt of the unconscious security guard who was lying at his feet and handed them to the bank manager.

"Find the one that opens the door!" he demanded.

The bank manager removed the key from the dangling set and handed it to Vega, who threw it to Cece so she could head out.

T.J., now behind the counter, forced all but one teller to the ground and handed her a duffle bag from under his arm.

"Empty the drawers and fill the bag, bitch!" he shouted.

Sonny beckoned the bank manager to the vault. As they walked through the swinging barrier, the bank manager glanced over his shoulder in an attempt to get a quick look-see of his assailant. Aware that he was eyeing him for a description, Sonny nudged him with the .45.

"Don't be a wise ass! Get going!"

The bank manager took heed to Sonny's command, and they arrived at the safe inside the vault.

"Open it!" Sonny demanded.

The bank manager kneeled down on one leg and nervously entered the combination numbers to the safe. Growing impatient, Sonny ordered him to move faster.

"What's taking you so fucking long?"

Again, the bank manager tried to look behind him, but Sonny nudged him with the gun for the second time.

"I can't concentrate with you pressing that thing in my back," he commented.

"Well, get used to it if you wanna live!" Sonny replied. "You got thirty seconds!"

Within seconds, the safe door opened. It was filled with safety deposit boxes and stacks of money secured with rubber bands. Sonny unfastened the clasp on the briefcase and handed it to the bank manager.

"Just the money!" he said.

The bank manager hurriedly filled the briefcase and fastened it. After taking it from him, Sonny ordered him to the ground. Then he backed out of the vault with his gun still pointed at the bank manager. T.J. and Vega, who stood with their guns covering the bank, witnessed Sonny as he came out.

"Let's move it!" Sonny yelled.

T.J. and Vega followed Sonny's lead and headed for the side exit. The security guard was now gaining consciousness, and through blurred vision, he grabbed Vega by the cuff of his pants as he tried to escape. Vega looked down and, to his surprise, found himself staring into the nose of a .25 revolver that the guard had lifted from his ankle holster. The security guard fired two shots into Vega's heart at point blank range. Vega died instantly.

Hearing the shots, Sonny turned back. He looked at Vega's slain body and then at the security guard, who dropped his gun at the sight of Sonny's menacing glare. T.J. grabbed Sonny by the arm.

"There's nothing we can do. He's already gone," T.J. told him.

Sonny stalled momentarily, but hearkened when T.J. tugged at his sleeve. Cece had the engine running. They fled through the exit and leapt into the opened cab door. After T.J. shut the door, Cece gunned the gas pedal and sped out of the parking lot.

The van turned at the corner and bumped a lamppost as it whipped by, causing it to fall over with a loud crash as it hit the pavement. Sonny and T.J. removed their disguises and tossed them into a large green trash bag, as Cece had already done. When Cece looked in the rearview mirror, she noticed Vega was missing.

"What happened to Chico?" she asked.

"His name is Vega, and he's no longer with us," Sonny replied.

"Oh well. More to go around, right?"

"How could you be so insensitive, Cece? A man just lost his life?" T.J. said with a disgusted tone.

"He got what he deserved, and I ain't like his ass anyway," Cece responded. "And by the way, where the fuck were you when I flashed the window blinds?"

"You flashed them, and I came right away. So what's your beef?"

"Don't lie. You were in there eating breakfast, you greedy bastard!"

"Oh, my bad. I was hungry," T.J. said.

They emptied the money and weapons into a knapsack and

dumped the briefcase into the trash bag. Sonny then climbed up front and sat beside Cece in the passenger seat.

The authorities had been alerted and were on the chase. Sonny spotted that they were being tailed, and he warned Cece.

"We got company."

Cece checked the mirror on her side and smiled confidently.

"Don't worry. I got this," she assured him.

She zipped through the moving traffic, made a sharp turn, and ducked into an alley. After the patrol car soared by, Cece shifted the van in reverse and then scooted forward. A second patrol car spotted the van from a distance and took pursuit. It chased them for several blocks before they came to a stoplight. Crossing the intersection, Cece came face to face with a speeding fuel truck that crossed her path. Sonny could feel his heart in his sleeve.

"Look out!" he yelled.

Cece whipped the van with a sharp right, missing the truck by a hair. The patrol car swerved from its course and was cut off.

Cece, now excited by the successful death-defying maneuver, belted out a victorious, "Yee-haw!"

Sonny wiped his forehead with a sigh of relief, leaned back in the seat, and turned to look at Cece.

"Are you out of your fucking mind? You almost got us killed!"

"What are you complaining for? We made it, didn't we?"

"Yeah, but that was too fucking close, not to mention the damage back there," Sonny said. "Let's keep it simple from here on, okay?"

"Look, Sonny, you asked me to do a job, and I'm doing it. Just sit back and enjoy the ride."

"Whatever, Cece. Just get us the hell away from here. We're already in enough trouble as it is. No more stunts."

"Aye-aye, Captain," Cece responded.

Minutes later, the van pulled beside an abandoned warehouse in a deserted lot along Bushwick Avenue. Sonny, Cece, and T.J.

climbed out. Holding a gas can, T.J. doused the interior and exterior of the van, then pulled a cigarette lighter from his pocket and tossed the lighter into the van before they took cover behind the building.

Within seconds, the van caught fire and erupted into a ball of flames. They looked at each other and smiled, convinced that all of the evidence leading to the crime had been eliminated.

Sonny swung the knapsack over his shoulder and disappeared into the warehouse for a dirt bike that had been stashed there overnight.

"We'll split up from here," he said, giving instructions to Cece and T.J. "The subway's a block ahead. Take the 'L' back to East New York. We'll meet up later at my place."

"That's what's up," Cece agreed.

"What about the money?" T.J. asked.

"You'll get your money, T.J. Chill," Sonny assured him.

"A'ight, man, we out," said T.J. as they gave each other dap.

Sonny started off on the bike, but stopped to give T.J. and Cece a fair warning.

"And remember, play it cool," he told them and then rode off.

Chapter 19

Home Free

The report of the bank robbery headlined all over the media throughout the duration of the midday hour. News journalists from every major network gave altered versions of the account, but all of the results were conclusive. Keisha watched intensely as the telecast reenacted from the 12-inch black and white television set in her living room.

"Police are asking the public for help in the arrests of three suspects for a heist that took place at the East New York Savings Bank on Atlantic Avenue this morning. Witnesses say a cleverly disguised African American woman, believed to be in her twenties, distracted bank associates while three heavily armed males forced the bank manager inside the vault and demanded money. One of the assailants, a Hispanic male with a prior criminal record identified as Luís Pablo Vega, was shot and killed during an attempt to escape. The others drove off in an untagged white van that was later found set ablaze, and got away with more than one hundred thousand in cash. The other two men involved were described as a husky black male wearing dark sunglasses and a minority in a ski mask. All three suspects are considered armed and dangerous. A ten thousand dollar reward has been offered for any information leading to their arrests."

Keisha turned the television off. She hadn't heard from Sonny since he left the house that morning, and the suspense was driving her crazy. On the bright side, the news kept her informed in case anyone got caught or hurt. But now, there was a price tag on the heads of her man, her only brother, and her best friend, and she couldn't bear to watch.

There was no way of getting in touch with the others to warn them of the danger they were in. Keisha now regretted bashing Sonny about their financial situation. After all, it wasn't his fault; he had tried doing things the right way. Sonny did everything in his power to find an honest job. He got up every morning to get the paper from the newsstand and search the want ads. He applied for each job he was qualified to do. He even applied for the jobs that were above his level of qualifications just to see if he could get a foot in the door. But, he was turned down everywhere he went, and every day was the same as the next one. *Sonny was right about one thing,* Keisha thought. *No one was going to hire him with his track record.* Still, she had no right to force his hand and send him on a suicide mission.

And what about Cece? she thought. That was her girl from way back. If anything were to happen to her, she would never be able to forgive herself.

T.J. was her own flesh and blood. There was no way on earth Keisha could ever explain to her parents how she allowed her brother to be talked into doing something illegal. They would strangle her first and ask questions later.

Keisha hadn't given up hope yet, though, and she couldn't because there was too much at stake. She had a family of her own to think about now, and the boys meant more to her than life itself. Even though she and Sonny's relationship wasn't as good as it could have been, Keisha still believed in him. If Sonny deserved credit for anything, it was for keeping his word. When Sonny promised something, he always came through no matter what.

Keisha could always count on that. It was just a matter of time before Sonny walked through the door and told her that everything was going to be okay. At least, that's what she was hoping for.

Disturbing thoughts continued to run through Keisha's mind, so she stretched out on the sofa to relax. Her youngest, Malik, had fallen asleep in her arms. Keisha cradled her baby's head in her hand and caressed it gently. She watched him lay like a cub in the comfort of its mother's care. Foster and Jahlil, who had been playing in the room with their fire trucks, both ran out.

"Mommy, can we eat now?" Foster asked while tapping on Keisha's knee.

Keisha had totally forgotten about feeding the kids their lunch that afternoon. She looked at the hanging pendulum clock on the wall. It was shaped in the image of a black cat, with moving eyes and an irritating tail that wagged back and forth all day long. Keisha hated the clock and wanted to take it down a long time ago, but Sonny insisted it stay up because it reminded him of the cartoon character Felix the Cat.

Keisha jumped at Foster's touch, nearly dropping Malik, but caught him just in time. However, he woke up crying from the sudden movement. She stands up.

"I know. I know," she said, standing up and patting him with care as his head rested on her shoulder. "Mommy's sorry, baby."

Keisha walked into the boys' bedroom and placed Malik on the bed with a bottle. He soon fell back to sleep. She came out of the room with a scowled expression, grabbed Foster, and shook him.

"Didn't I tell you about sneaking up on me? I would have torn your behind up if you made me drop my baby!" she said angrily.

Foster sadly lowered his head.

"Come here," Keisha said, pulling him to her bosom. "Mommy didn't mean to yell at you. She has a lot on her mind, okay?" She gave him a motherly hug and kiss.

"What's wrong, Mommy?" Foster asked, seeing she was upset.

122

"It's nothing, baby. Just grown-up stuff," she replied.

"Then can we eat now?"

Foster's innocence made Keisha smile. She looked over at Jahlil, who had been standing quietly in the corner, hoping Keisha didn't jump on him next.

"Are you hungry too, big head?" she asked.

"Yes, Auntie," he answered.

"Well, c'mon then. Let's go see what we can find in the kitchen."

Keisha entered the kitchen with the boys and tossed a can of spaghetti and meatballs into a pot. Her nerves were too upset to eat anything, so she sat with the boys at the table and watched them. Her heart jumped when she heard a series of loud banging at the front door. Keisha ran and looked through the peephole. It was Sonny. She opened the door.

"Hi, Sonny!" the boys cried from the table.

"Sonny, thank God you're alive," Keisha said excitedly.

Sonny burst in, pushing Keisha aside and almost knocking her into the wall. He stormed into the bedroom, where he dropped the knapsack. Keisha ran after him. Beads of sweat rolled off Sonny's body as he tore his shirt off and sat on the bed. He wiped himself with the garment and looked at Keisha.

"Get me something to drink," he said.

"Where's T.J. and Cece? Are they alright?" Keisha asked.

"They're fine, Keisha. I just saw them coming up the street. Now can you please get me something to drink? I'm dying of thirst!"

Keisha went to the window and stuck her head out. "Are you sure? I don't see them."

"Keisha!" Sonny yelled.

"Okay, I heard you."

Keisha rushed to the kitchen for Sonny's drink. When she returned, Sonny was sprawled out on the bed.

"Here you go, baby," she said, handing Sonny a glass of cherry Kool-Aid.

Sonny sat up. "Finally," he said, then drank the Kool-Aid in one gulp.

Keisha placed the empty glass on the dresser.

"Now tell me what happened. I've been worried sick. The robbery was all over the news, Sonny," she said.

"Everything blew up in our faces," Sonny admitted. "The timing was fucked up, and Vega...he's dead!" He slumped over, palming his face with his hands.

"I know," Keisha said. She stroked the back of Sonny's head to console him. "But, it wasn't your fault. He knew the risks of taking this job before he got into it, so don't go blaming yourself."

Sonny looked up and removed Keisha's hand. "Is that what you would've said had it been me?"

"Of course not. How could you say something like that?" Keisha asked. "I haven't had a moments rest since you left."

Sonny got up and held her. "I know that, baby. I didn't mean it. This has just been one fucked up day." Sonny picked up the knapsack and opened it. "But, we made out like bandits. Look at this."

He pulled out the one .45 that he saved and sat it on the nightstand. Then, he turned the bag upside down and emptied the loot onto the bed. Keisha almost fainted at the sight of the money.

"Oh my God, look at all that money!" she said. "So this is what a hundred thousand dollars looks like, huh?"

"It's probably close to that, give or take a few dollars," Sonny guessed.

"No, it's really a hundred thousand, Sonny. That's the sum they reported on the news."

Sonny looked at the money. "Then it was well worth it. We're rich, baby!" He swept Keisha off her feet and spun her around.

Just then, Foster ran into the bedroom and yelled out,

"Someone's at the door!"

Sonny covered Foster's mouth and shushed him.

"Who do you think it is?" Keisha asked.

"How should I know?" Sonny replied, while wrapping the bed sheets over the money.

He tossed it in the closet and grabbed the .45. They tipped to the kitchen to get Jahlil and then put the boys in their bedroom. Sonny followed Keisha to the front door, carrying the .45 behind his back.

"Answer it," he said, nudging Keisha.

"Stop pushing on me," she whispered.

Keisha turned the covering over the peephole slowly. She peeked through. Standing in the hall on the other side of the door was her brother and best friend.

"It's Cece and T.J.," she said.

"Is anybody else with them?" Sonny asked.

"No, I don't think so."

"Okay, then open it."

Keisha slid the security bar away from the door and unlocked it.

"What the hell took y'all so long?" Cece asked, barging in.

Keisha bolted the door.

"Making sure you wasn't Five-0," Sonny said. "Grab a chair and come to the back."

They followed Sonny and spread about the bedroom.

"Can I get something to drink, sis?" T.J. asked. "I'm burning up."

"Yeah, but you better get it yourself, if you know like I know," Keisha replied.

"T.J., bring me one, too," Cece added, fanning her t-shirt.

Keisha was standing in the doorway. T.J. hugged her as he passed by.

"Ugh! Get your hot, sweaty behind off me!" she said, pushing

125

him off her. "And wash your hands!"

As T.J. went for the drinks, everyone sat silently until he got back. He handed Cece a beverage when he returned.

"So what I miss?" he asked.

"Nothing. We were waiting on you," Sonny told him. "And now that you're here, let's get this thing over with."

Sonny went into the closet for the money and threw it on the bed. The greed came out of Cece and T.J. They screamed in excitement.

"Jackpot!" Cece yelled.

"Yeah, buddy!" T.J. added.

"Y'all gonna let the whole fucking building know our business," Sonny said. "Keep it down!"

He started to divide the money stacks into rows. T.J. and Cece watched closely as he counted.

"That's seventy-five thousand dollars even," Sonny said. "Those fucking crooks at the bank lied out their asses."

"What do you mean, Sonny?" Cece asked, becoming suspicious.

"The robbery was on the news," Keisha said. "They claim y'all got away with over a hundred thousand dollars."

"I'm just glad it's all over with," T.J. said. "How much is that divided by three?"

"That's twenty-five thousand dollars apiece, Einstein," Cece arrogantly stated.

"See, nobody was talking to you, Cece. So, mind your business," T.J. barked.

Sonny walked out of the room and returned with a large brown paper bag that he put a third of the cash in. He put another part of the money in the knapsack. Before doing so, he gave Cece her cut first.

"Here you go, Cece," he said, handing her the paper bag. You're going right upstairs, so this'll do."

126

T.J. stretched his hand out.

"Hot damn, boy! You ready, ain't you?" Sonny joked, giving T.J. his cut. "Don't go spending it all in one place now."

T.J. unzipped the side compartments of the bag. He sulked when he saw they were all empty.

"Yo, where's my burner?" he asked, looking at Sonny.

"I got rid of it before I got here, and it wasn't yours to begin with," Sonny stated. "You better take this money and be happy, nigga."

Cece stood up from the bed and stretched. "Let me head on upstairs and get my outfit ready for tonight. It's time to celebrate! Can I leave Jahlil with y'all?"

"You're joking, right?" Sonny asked, enraged. "We just robbed a fucking bank. Nobody's going anywhere but home! We've got to lay low for a while, and that means no showboating. For the time being, spend only as much as you need. We don't want to draw any attention."

"So how long are we supposed to wait, Sonny?" Cece asked. "I mean, damn, what's the point of having the money if we can't spend it?"

"Just a couple of weeks, give or take. Everybody will have forgotten about this shit by that time."

"Alright, I guess so," Cece said, accepting the terms.

"I'm cool with that," T.J. agreed.

"Good. Now you're both talking with some sense," Sonny told them.

Keisha let Cece out, but allowed Jahlil to stay with her since he was napping. She called a taxicab for T.J. Sonny walked him downstairs when the cab arrived.

"I'll holler at you later, bro," he told Sonny as he got into the backseat.

"Fo' sho," Sonny replied. "And don't make any detours. Go straight home."

Patron Gold

Chapter 20

Hood Rich

Keisha and Sonny stayed glued to the television set that night. The bank story continued to heighten in the media, but there were no indications stating the authorities had any leads to the crime. When they finally went to bed, Sonny fell asleep as soon as his head hit the pillow. Keisha, on the other hand, tossed and turned for most of the night.

For the next couple of days, countless numbers of witnesses came forward with false testimonies, trying to claim the reward money. Within a week, the hype of the robbery died down, and everything went back to normal. Now it was time to celebrate.

The first thing Keisha and Sonny did with their newfound riches was catch up on all of their unpaid bills. The landlord was surprised when Keisha showed up at his front door with the past due rent. He already had the date marked on his calendar to evict them so he could paint the apartment and rent it out to another family at a higher rate. However, he greedily accepted the money plus two months' rent in advance when Keisha handed it to him. After the bills were taken care of, Keisha and Sonny redecorated the whole apartment with brand-new furniture from the most expensive manufacturers in town. Sonny also added a state-of-the-art stereo system with wall-to-wall speakers to go with the new look for the living room. The entire family got new wardrobes from the latest fashion designers. They were the envy of the neighborhood.

Cece lived life to the fullest, and she enjoyed it. She partied every night and recuperated just enough to do it all over again the next day. Like Keisha, she got out of debt, paid her bills up to date, and refurnished her apartment. And Jahlil, of course, was dressed to impress. She even took care of her mother Clara by purchasing groceries and dropped her a few dollars every week without being too conspicuous. Clara took the money without questioning where it came from, and let Cece go about her business.

T.J. was careless and ran through his loot quickly. He lived like a baller in the VIP room at the strip clubs, sipping on Moet and paying for lap dances. He also blew a stack a night taking the strippers back to a motel room for a private show and sex. Within a week, T.J. was down to a couple of grand, but that didn't stop him from "making it rain" on them hoes.

Chapter 21

The Block is Hot

Things were starting to look up. Everybody was happy, and nobody worried about money because the money was there. But nothing lasts forever; eventually, all things come to an end.

It was a Thursday afternoon, the beginning of the Fourth of July weekend. Sonny and Keisha celebrated the holiday by throwing a huge cookout for the entire neighborhood. It was held in the courtyard behind the building, but anybody who came through was more than welcome to participate. Sonny spent nearly five hundred dollars having the food catered and a few hundred more on beer kegs. Cece hired a deejay from one of the clubs where she partied. It was a joyful event. The grownups drank and held spades tournaments, with wagers placed on each game. Sonny turned the fire hydrant on so the kids could cool off. They splashed under the water and sprayed the cars that passed by. A few cars slowed down to get the free wash, but some of the old players who rolled with their tops down didn't appreciate the water. The kids sprayed them anyway and got cussed out, but it was all in good fun. That lasted for a while, until the police came with the big wrench and shut the hydrant off.

The number of heads at the cookout started to decrease by nightfall. However, that didn't stop the party. The spades tournament continued. Only now the teams were separated by genre: the women at one table and the men at another. In the final round, each winning team would play the other in a battle of the sexes faceoff for the championship. The prize was five hundred dollars in cash and a trophy cup for each team member.

A familiar sound blasted from the tweeters of a blue and white vehicle that cruised through the block. It was the Mr. Softee ice cream truck. As the enticing jingle lured them in, all of the neighborhood children dropped what they were doing and searched their pockets frantically for loose change. Foster and Jahlil ran up to Sonny at the card table with Malik trailing behind.

"Sonny, the ice cream man is here. Can we have a dollar?" Foster begged.

"Hang on for a second, fellas," Sonny said, addressing the men at the table. He unfolded a wad of bills from his money clip.

Gates, a big burly cat, spoke up. "Hey, man, I'm trying to make money and you taking money. Can't you send them crumb snatchers to they mammy?"

Reaching across the table, Sonny snatched Gates by the collar, withdrew the .45 from his waist, and stuck it against Gates' nose. Gates nearly shit on himself as the cold steel probed his nostrils.

"Look, you bitch-ass nigga, nobody asked for your fucking advice. And if you ever disrespect my woman or kids again, I'll make you eat this shit. Now do we understand each other, punk?"

"Yeah, man. I ain't mean no harm," Gates responded apologetically.

"Yeah, that's what I thought," Sonny said, putting the gun away. Then, turning his attention back to Foster, he gave him three dollars and told him to hold his brother's hand as they took off for the ice cream truck.

*****

Keisha and Cece had gone to the corner store to get more ice for the coolers and were just returning. As they got midway up the block, they noticed a crowd gathered in the middle of the street, but could not make out what was happening. As they got closer, Cece spotted Sonny's figure. She could see he was kneeling over someone.

"Oh my God, Keisha, that's Sonny!" she yelled.

Both women took off running in Sonny's direction. Keisha's heart skipped a beat when she noticed Malik's body lying in the street.

"My baby! Sonny, what happened to my baby?" she screamed.

Malik's eyes were closed, and he wasn't moving. Sonny had taken his shirt off, and propped it under Malik's head.

"He was hit by a car, but he's going to be fine, baby," Sonny reassured her. "Just stay calm."

"But how did this happen? What was Malik doing in the street?"

Foster ran into Keisha's arms. "He let go of my hand and ran around the ice cream truck, Mommy. I tried to stop him," he cried.

"It's not your fault, baby," Keisha said, comforting him with a hug. Then she turned to Sonny. "Sonny, you knew Cece and I were going to the store. Couldn't you keep an eye on the boys until I got back?"

"I did keep an eye on them, Keisha, but you know how kids are. Accidents happen."

"Yeah, right. I bet you didn't budge from that card table the whole time I was gone."

"What are you trying to say? Do you think I meant for this to happen?"

"I'm saying you could be a little more responsible when it comes to the children, Sonny. Did you at least call an ambulance?"

"Yes, Keisha. There's one on its way."

*****

At the hospital, Sonny and Keisha sat side by side in the waiting room area. Malik was still unconscious when they arrived in the ambulance, but there had been no change in his condition. Keisha was a nervous wreck. Someone had to tell her something about her baby or she would lose it. She walked to the nurse's station.

"Has he opened his eyes yet?" she asked for the fifth time.

"I'm afraid not, but the doctors are doing all they can," the nurse replied.

Keisha was steaming. "Why is it taking you people so long to help my child? We'd have been out of here by now had it been a white baby in there!"

Sonny got up and apologized for Keisha's outburst. "Please excuse my wife. She isn't taking this very well."

"I understand, sir. I will let you know when I hear something," the nurse responded.

"Thank you."

Sonny led Keisha back to her seat. She was in tears and concerned for Malik's welfare. He put an arm around her.

"You're going to get us kicked out of here with that mouth before we hear anything from the doctor."

"But why won't they let us go inside? I'm his mother. I have a right to be with my baby."

"Keisha, there's nothing we can do but sit here and wait. The doctors are doing what they can to make him better. Now stop worrying, okay?"

"I'll try," Keisha answered.

"Good," Sonny replied. "Now I don't know how long we're going to be here, so I'm going for a cup of coffee. Can I get you anything?"

"Yes. Get me a ginger ale, please."

"Alright. Don't go anywhere. I'll be right back," Sonny said humorously.

"Hurry back, baby," Keisha said with a smile.

Detectives O'Reilly and Flanagan surfaced from the opposite side of the waiting room. They had been watching Sonny and Keisha the entire time. In fact, they had followed the ambulance that carried Malik to the hospital when the 911 call came in.

As it turned out, T.J. was identified as one of the accomplices in the bank robbery and had already been taken into custody. T.J. basically gave himself up by flashing his money around town, so it wasn't hard to find him when the search party began. The police caught up with him at a Motel 8 entertaining a stripper or vise-versa. He immediately cut a deal and voluntarily offered the information leading to Sonny and Cece's whereabouts. When Sonny was out of sight, the detectives approached Keisha.

"Keisha Johnson?" Flanagan asked.

"May I ask who wants to know?"

"I'm Detective Harry Flanagan." He flashed his badge. "And this is my partner, Detective O'Reilly."

O'Reilly tipped his hat upon the introduction.

"I'm Keisha Johnson. Is there a problem, Detective?"

"Mind if we take a seat?"

"No, be my guest," Keisha replied reluctantly.

"We answered the call when your son, Malik, was brought in. How's he doing?"

"Oh," Keisha said relieved. "Nothing has changed so far. He isn't responding, but he's in stable condition at least."

"Well, that's good to hear. I'm sure he's going to be just fine, Ms. Johnson," Flanagan said.

"Thank you. I sure hope so," Keisha answered.

Sonny, who was on his way back from the cafeteria, slowed his pace when he saw Flanagan and O'Reilly sitting with Keisha. He could smell a pig from a mile away. Sonny had two options. He could turn and make a run for it, or he could face his penalty like a man. Sonny thought about it. Running would only get Keisha involved. They would harass her just to get to him. He guessed at what he thought his sentence would be. He was probably looking at eight to ten years for armed robbery. The boys would practically be grown by then. Sonny wanted Foster and Malik to be men who lived up to their expectations. However, now the odds were against them. A young man could easily be led astray without the guidance of a father in his life, and Sonny knew that all too well. His own father abandoned him when he was growing up, and now he was about to do the same thing to Malik. *At least they still have Keisha,* he thought.

Sonny walked forward. O'Reilly moved down a seat, letting him sit next to Keisha. Sonny handed Keisha the soda.

"Here's the man of the hour," O'Reilly remarked.

"Sonny," Keisha began, "these gentlemen are from the police department. They came to see how Malik is doing."

Sonny looked at Keisha and asked, "Did you tell them anything?"

"Tell them about what? I don't understand."

Flanagan stood up and displayed his badge. "Sonny Blake, you're under arrest for armed robbery," he said while removing a pair of cuffs from his belt.

O'Reilly removed his gun from its holster and stuck it into Sonny's side. "Stand up. And don't try any funny shit, or I'll blow a hole right through you," he threatened.

"Ma'am, I'm going to need you to step aside," Flanagan added.

Sonny stood and placed his hands behind his back as he was instructed. When he was cuffed, O'Reilly and Flanagan led him out of the emergency room and into the parking lot.

Keisha followed as they escorted Sonny to an unmarked vehicle.

"Sonny!" she yelled at the top of her lungs.

"Keisha, go back inside!" he shouted, looking back.

O'Reilly gave Sonny a shove. "I wouldn't be worrying about her if I were you, lover boy. You're going away for a long, long time. In a month, she'll forget all about you and give that sweet black pussy to some other nigger stud!"

Sonny broke free from the detectives. "Fuck you, pig!" he said and spat in O'Reilly's face.

Flanagan regained hold of him.

O'Reilly wiped his mug. "You fucking coon, I'm gonna kill you!" he screamed, pinning Sonny against the car. He began choking him.

"Motherfucker!" Keisha yelled, running towards the car.

When O'Reilly turned around, Keisha lunged at him with a blow that landed on his jaw. O'Reilly stumbled back and fell to the ground.

"Why, you little bitch!" he said, getting to his feet. He drew his hand back to strike at Keisha, but Flanagan caught his arm. Keisha ran to Sonny's side.

"John, are you nuts? That's a woman!" Flanagan said. "We got who we came for. Now let's take him and be on our way."

Keisha held onto Sonny and kissed him. "I'll come down and get you out of there just as soon as I can," she promised.

"Don't worry about me, baby. I'll be fine. You stay here and see that they take good care of our son," Sonny told her.

"Okay," Keisha answered tearfully.

"I love you, Keisha. Wait for me."

"I love you, too, Sonny, and I will," she replied.

Flanagan placed Sonny in the back of the squad car while O'Reilly made his way to the front. Keisha wasn't about to get him again. He watched her like a hawk as he backed towards the driver's side with his finger on the trigger of the .38 on his hip.

As Keisha watched Sonny being taken away, an eerie feeling of déjà vu sunk in. She recalled a related experience awhile back with

Detroit. Only now it was happening with Sonny. Too much for Keisha to bear, anxiety kicked in. A sense of breathlessness extended to choking, and her eyes got blurry. Before Keisha could figure out what was happening, she passed out in the middle of the parking lot. It was fortunate that someone witnessed the incident and reported it to the triage station. When Keisha regained consciousness, she found herself stretched out on a gurney in one of the hospital rooms. She looked up to find a nurse standing over her. The nurse took Keisha's pulse.

"Where am I, and where's my baby?" Keisha asked.

"Here I am, Mommy," Malik answered, smiling from across the room.

"Malik!" Keisha screamed excitedly. She tried to get up, but the nurse stopped her.

"Relax, Ms. Johnson. You shouldn't move so quickly just yet," she said.

Keisha felt the back of her head where a knot had developed. "What the hell...what happened?" she asked.

"You had a nasty fall, Ms. Johnson. You fainted in the parking lot."

The news came as a bit of a shock to Keisha because she had no recollection of anything that had happened after the detectives took Sonny away. However, she did understand why the accident occurred; she was stressed out.

Keisha got to her feet and pushed the nurse aside as she ran to Malik.

"Hi, baby. Mommy's so glad to see you." She embraced Malik and smothered him with kisses.

"Ms. Johnson, it is advisable that you lay down. You've suffered a mild concussion. The doctor wants to run a few tests—"

Keisha cut the nurse off. "How is my baby? Is everything okay with him?"

"Your son is fine, Ms. Johnson. He's got a few scrapes and

138

bruises, but that's all. On the other hand, you really should come lay—"

Keisha interrupted her for a second time. "As long as my baby is fine, I'm okay," she answered. "When can I take him home?"

"He'll have to stay overnight, but if he continues to show improvement, you can take him home tomorrow."

"Then I'll be staying with him. He's never spent a night away from home."

"I'm sure that wouldn't be a problem, Ms. Johnson," the nurse replied. "I'll make the arrangements for your stay."

"Thank you," Keisha said and sat down. "Oh shit," she blurted out abruptly.

It had just dawned on Keisha that the detectives would soon be coming for T.J. and Cece next, unless they had already done so. Maybe there was still some chance of hope. Keisha had to warn them regardless. She looked around the room, but there was no phone.

"Is there something wrong, Ms. Johnson?" the nurse asked.

"Yes, there is," Keisha replied. "I have another son who's with the babysitter. I'll have to let her know I won't be coming home tonight. Could you sit with my son while I give her a call?"

"Sure, Ms. Johnson, I would be glad to." the nurse answered. "There's a payphone down the hall. Make a left as you go out of the room."

"Thank you. I'll be right back," Keisha said.

"You're welcome, and take your time. There's no rush."

Keisha ran down the hospital corridor while fumbling through her purse for change to use the payphone. When she got into the small booth, she dialed her parents' number first, hoping T.J. was at home. Victoria picked up when the phone rang.

"Hello, Johnson residence."

"Hi, Mama. It's me...Keisha. Is T.J. there?" she asked, out of breath.

"Keisha, I've been trying to get in touch with you all night, but Cece said you were still at the hospital. How is Malik doing?" Victoria asked.

"He's doing fine, Mama. He just woke up a little while ago. But where is T.J.?"

"Keisha, that brother of yours has gotten himself into a world of trouble," Victoria stated heartbrokenly. "The police arrested him sometime earlier today. He's in jail. They said he was involved in that bank robbery. Did you know anything about this?"

Keisha wanted to claim that she had no idea of T.J.'s involvement with the bank robbery, but she couldn't. The truth was already out in the open. It would only make matters worse by lying to Victoria. Besides, Sonny had been caught, too. By now, he and T.J. were more than likely sharing the same cell. *It was probably my brother's dumb ass who sold Sonny out,* Keisha thought.

"Yes, Mama, I knew about it," she confessed.

"Keisha, I can't believe what I'm hearing. You knew about this all along and didn't say anything? Who else was involved?"

"Sonny and Cece helped him, Mama. They were all in it together," Keisha painfully confessed. "The police came by the hospital and picked Sonny up not too long ago."

"Oh my God, Keisha. Are you alright?"

"I'm fine, Mama," she replied.

"Well, thank goodness for that," Victoria said. "I swear, Keisha, between you and your brother, I don't know who's going to send me to my grave first. It's like y'all are having a contest to see which one will outdo the other. I just don't understand. Where did your father and I go wrong?"

"You did nothing wrong, Mama. You and Daddy were great parents, and I'm sorry you feel that way. But, I can't talk to you right now. I need to call Cece."

"This is going to break poor Clara's heart when she finds out. She's having a hard enough time as it is dealing with her health,"

Victoria commented.

"Mama, I hate to cut you short, but I have to hang up now. I'll call you back as soon as I can."

"Wait, Keisha. Who has Foster?"

"I left him with Cece, Mama. That's why I have to go. Bye."

Keisha hung up on Victoria and immediately dialed the number for Cece, who had just come in the house with the boys.

"Hello," she said, answering the call.

"Cece, Sonny and T.J. got busted. You have to get out of there!" Keisha revealed.

"Oh shit! Are you serious? Is Malik okay?" Cece asked.

"Yes, he's fine, but you're not listening to me. They'll be coming for you next. Pack what you can and take the boys to my parents' house. And hurry."

"Okay, and thanks, Keisha. I don't know where I'm going, but I've gotta lay low. I'll get in touch with you when I think it's safe."

"Alright. Now get out of there already."

"I am," Cece replied. "Keisha, I need you to do something for me."

"What is it?"

Cece's voice trembled. "You know that you're my best friend in the whole world. I mean, you and I go way back."

"Yes, Cece, but what are you getting at?"

"Mama's getting old. If for some reason I don't make it, promise me that you'll look out for Jahlil."

"You know I will. I'm his godmother. Why are you even talking like that, Cece? You're scaring me."

"I'm not sure, Keisha. I just have a bad feeling about this. But, enough with this mushy stuff. I've gotta get going. Take care, sis. I love you."

Keisha choked on her words, but managed to get them out. "I love you, too, sis. Be safe."

Chapter 22

On the Run

Cece ran into her bedroom to retrieve her stash hidden in a leather shoulder bag beneath a pile of dirty clothes in the back of the closet. She dug the bag out and counted her stacks. There was a little over ten thousand dollars remaining from what she had already spent.

Cece threw the bag on her shoulder and left the room. She wanted to grab a few things for Jahlil, but there wasn't enough time. The police were probably on their way to her apartment, so she had to get out as quickly as possible. The boys were in the kitchen eating leftover burgers from a plate that Cece had brought upstairs from the cookout. Cece called for them as she unlocked the front door.

"Jahlil and Foster, stop what you're doing! We have to go!"

"But, Mommy, we ain't finished eating yet," Jahlil blurted.

Cece was tempted to snatch Jahlil from the table and drag him to the door, but she withheld from doing so. This would probably be the last time she saw her son for a long time, and she wanted to leave him with a good impression.

"Jahlil, please don't argue with me right now. I'm not in the mood. I told you to come on. Now let's go."

"Yes, ma'am," he replied.

The boys rushed past Cece and ran into the hall. Cece looked around the apartment one last time while standing in the doorway. She wished there were a way she could turn back the hands of time, but that was a seemingly hopeless situation. She had a better chance at trapping a leprechaun with a pot of gold. So, Cece shut the door and locked it on the way out.

Cece and the boys headed down the stairs. When they reached the bottom floor, three marked patrol cars pulled up to the front of the building. Cece had to think fast. She grabbed Jahlil and Foster by their hands and hurried to the courtyard. They fought their way through the crowd of people who were still celebrating the holiday, and made it to the cellar exit that led to the other side of the street.

Cece peeked above the ground at the top of the landing to make sure the coast was clear before they went up. There were no signs of the police, so they made a run for it. When they reached the corner, Cece hailed a cab and had the driver take her to Keisha's parents' home. She paid the fare, tipping him twenty dollars extra, and asked him to wait on her. He agreed.

Victoria inched the drapes to the side and peered through the dining room window when she heard the cab pull up. When she saw that it was Cece, she went to open the door, but Thomas jumped ahead of her.

"I'll get it," he said, brushing her aside.

"Hi, Grandpa," Foster said, pushing his way in and hugging Thomas around the waist.

"Hey, sport. How's Grandpa's favorite little man? You been a good boy?"

"Yes, sir. Does that mean I get a reward?" Foster asked anxiously.

"It sure does," Thomas answered. "Go in the kitchen and tell your grandma I said to give you a great big bowl of ice cream."

"Yay!" Foster yelled as he ran past him.

Thomas turned his attention towards Cece. "Thanks for

bringing the boy, but you'd better get going now. The police done already been here once. Ain't no sense in them coming back."

"I'm going, Mr. Thomas, but can I please leave Jahlil with you and Ms. Victoria?" Cece pleaded.

"Excuse me? Your mama lives right up the street. Why can't you take him there? I done told you we don't want to be involved in this mess. If it wasn't for Foster, I wouldn't have let you in."

"Please, Mr. Thomas. I got a cab waiting outside, and the meter's running," Cece begged.

"And why should that bother you, Queen Bee? You got money," Thomas cracked.

Victoria, who had been standing behind him the whole time listening in on the conversation, came to Cece's aid.

"Thomas, stop being so mean. You know the girl is in trouble," she said in Cece's defense. "Cece, you can leave Jahlil here with us. I'll call Clara and let her know."

"Thank you so much, Ms. Victoria, you don't know how much this means to me," Cece said thankfully. Then she got down on one knee and spoke to Jahlil. "Listen, baby," she began. "Mommy has to go away and take care of some business. I want you to promise me that you'll be a good boy and behave yourself while I'm gone. Don't be giving Ms. Victoria no trouble. You hear me?"

"Yes, Mommy, I promise," Jahlil said. "Are you coming back to pick me up in the morning?"

Cece fought to hold back the tears. "No, baby, not in the morning. But, I'll come back to get you real soon, okay?"

"Ok, Mommy."

Cece embraced Jahlil, holding onto him as though it were the last time she would ever see him. When she turned him loose, he looked up at Victoria.

"May I go and have ice cream now?" he asked.

"You sure can, sweetie," Victoria answered. "Now, you run and have a seat with Foster while I talk to your mommy. I'll be

145

there in just a minute."

"Yes, ma'am," Jahlil said. He hugged Cece once more and then ran off to the kitchen.

The cab driver honked from outside.

"Well, I guess this is it," Cece said. She let the shoulder bag slide down her arm and reached inside to remove a stack of money that she handed to Victoria. "Ms. Victoria, I know you don't approve of this, but it's for Jahlil. Can you give it to Keisha? She'll know what to do."

"Yes, Cece, I understand. I'll hold onto this and give it to Keisha just as soon as I see her."

"Thank you again, Ms. Victoria."

"You're welcome, Cece, and may God be with you," Victoria replied as they embraced.

Cece hurried through the Johnson's front yard and opened the gate. She looked at the empty space near the curb where the cab should have been parked. Instead, she saw the driver taking off without her. Cece chased the cab down, but the heartless driver stared through his window and kept going. She banged on the trunk of the car and cursed him out as he sped down the street.

"You bastard! I hope your stank ass runs off the side of a bridge and die!"

Cece continued in the same direction, walking three long blocks, but there wasn't a cab in sight. She walked further until she came to the subway station on Rockaway Avenue. From there, she would take the #3 train to Penn Station and then catch the E train to JFK Airport. Cece proceeded to climb the platform steps, but turned and did an immediate about-face when she spotted the two transit officers that were posted at the top of the landing. She trotted back down the steps and stopped at the corner. Cece contemplated her next move while waiting for the traffic light to change. Her concentration was broken when a silver Audi Coupé pulled up.

A brown complexioned brother lowered the window and stuck his head out. It is K'shon, a dealer from the neighborhood who also happened to be Cece's main supplier. He had a thing for Cece, and she knew it. Whenever Cece came up short for drugs, he gave her credit, and when she borrowed money from him, she never paid it back. In Cece's mind, she was getting over on K'shon, but he considered it an investment. *One day she'll give in, and it'll be a wrap,* he always thought.

"What's good, sexy!" he shouted over the loud music coming from inside.

Cece walked up to the car. "Yo, turn your system down," she said as she leaned on the door. "I'm so glad to see you, boo. I need a ride. Can you help me out?" she asked flirtatiously.

"Yeah, I'm your boo when you need something. That's some wacked shit, Cece. When you gonna start being nice to a nigga?"

"Look, K'shon, I really need this favor. Look out for me this last time. I got you."

"That's better. Get in," K'shon said.

After letting Cece in his ride, he started the car up and pulled off.

"So where are we going, baby?" he asked.

Cece placed the shoulder bag in her lap. She then reached inside it and removed half a stack. K'shon's eyes widened when he saw how much Cece was holding.

"Damn, girl, what you do, rob a bank?"

"Take me to JFK Airport. This is for you," was all Cece said.

K'shon suddenly remembered hearing about a bank robbery some weeks back. He knew Sonny and T.J. were involved because they had just been caught. The word had spread all through the hood. But, he never imagined in his wildest dreams that Cece was the female counterpart the police were looking for. Yet, it all made sense. What other reason could she have for wanting him to take her to the airport?

K'shon bided for some time. Somehow, he was going to be a whole lot richer by the end of the night, and at Cece's expense.

"Shit, since you rolling like that, we might as well get lit," he said, opening the glove compartment.

He reached inside and pulled out an ounce of cocaine sealed in a Ziploc bag. Cece's eyes lit up like a kid in a candy store. The sight of the blow caused her heart to race. She was under a lot of pressure, and a one on one would definitely help calm her nerves, she decided.

"Damn, K'shon, where you get that?"

"You happy now, ain't you? But why are you so surprised? You know I keeps it poppin', baby!"

Cece was feening hard now. She knew it was in her best interest to get to the airport as soon as possible, but she had to get at least one hit in for now.

"You gonna let me have some, right?"

"Yeah, I guess I can break you off a little something. That's if you were serious about what you said."

Cece knew exactly what K'shon was talking about. He wanted sex. She tried to avoid the issue by offering more money.

"K'shon, I'm in a hurry. Can't you just sell a little to me? I don't want that much."

"See, there you go frontin' on a nigga again. I don't even know why I bother wasting my time fucking with you skeezin'-ass bitches," K'shon said, folding the Ziploc bag.

He whipped the car abruptly and pulled to the curb. He then reached over Cece's lap and opened the door on her side.

"Get the fuck out of my car!" he yelled.

Cece gave him a puzzled look. "Hold up, I just gave you five hundred dollars, K'shon. Why you tripping?"

"It ain't about the money. You know what I'm talking about. Look at all the times I done hooked you up, Cece. And for what, a fucking smile? It ain't even going down like that no more. You

148

either wit' it or you out."

"Okay, but you gotta be quick about it. I don't have all night," Cece said, giving into K'shon's demands. "And you're taking me straight to the airport afterwards, right?"

"It's your call, baby."

K'shon drove to a cheap motel nearby. When they got there, Cece went into the lobby and rented a room at the front desk, while K'shon waited for her in the car. When Cece came out with the key, she waved for K'shon, and he followed her in. Cece didn't waste any time once they were inside the room. She wanted the blow that K'shon promised, and she needed to get back on the road.

Cece pushed K'shon onto the bed and unzipped his pants. K'shon was intimidated by Cece's dominance, but it didn't matter to him. He had waited long for this moment to happen, and now his wish was finally coming true. Cece attacked K'shon's manhood with the aggression of a porn star with her head game. Within minutes, she had K'shon's toes curling, and his body trembled as if he were going into convulsions. Without warning, K'shon mushed Cece in the forehead and pulled out, shooting his load upward and into her eye.

Cece jumped up from the bed. "Ah shit!" she yelled, rushing to the bathroom.

She cleaned her face with soap and warm water, and dried off with a hand towel. When she returned to the room, the front door was open, and K'shon was gone. Cece rushed to the bedside where she had set her shoulder bag on the floor, praying it was still there, but it wasn't.

"That dirty motherfucker!" she screamed.

The sound of the Coupés engine roared from the outside. Cece ran towards the front door in an attempt to catch K'shon before he got away, but she halted when two federal agents and two uniformed officers stormed in aiming their guns at her. The front desk clerk, who matched Cece's face with the sketching of a mug shot that appeared on the news, called 911. Cece was frisked and then handcuffed. She cursed K'shon under her breath as the officers took her into custody.

*****

On the morning of September 15, 1980, Sonny Blake, Thomas Johnson Jr., and Cece Harris stood before a grand jury and awaited their arraignment. Cece was the first to receive a verdict. Her mother Clara was there for support. She refinanced the house in order to get Cece the best criminal defense lawyer that money could buy. When Clara saw her only daughter being led into the courtroom in shackles, she suffered from respiratory complications and was taken to the hospital for medical attention before the trial even began. However, Cece's lawyer handled the case very well. As a first-time offender, he was able to get Cece the minimal sentence of one to three years.

T.J.'s plea bargain did not hold up in court when it came time for his indictment. He was given five years for his part in the robbery. Thomas shook his head in disgust when his son was led out of the courtroom by the bailiffs. He wondered why he even bothered listening to Victoria and let her drag him downtown on his day off in the first place, especially since he had given up on T.J. a long time ago.

Sonny braced himself, expecting to face the worst conviction when it was time to accept his judgment. He was sure the jury would hang him because he was a repeat offender. They wouldn't understand that he committed the crime only to ensure that his family was provided for when all else had failed. He was sentenced to serve a maximum of ten years without the possibility of early parole.

Keisha had been unable to attend the hearing to see Sonny before he was sentenced because she did Clara the favor of watching Jahlil on Cece's behalf, and then there was no one left to watch Foster and Malik since both of her parents had gone, also. However, she did see Sonny thereafter. Every weekend, Keisha prepared for the long journey that started in Brooklyn and ended in Queens at Rikers Island, where she would sit and talk with him during visiting hours.

Keisha adapted to being on her own again, but this time, maturity contributed as a factor in her adjustment. When she first met Detroit and fell in love with him, she was just a young naïve girl who hadn't been out in the world. And there was no closure on the relationship when they broke up. Detroit just walked out of her life and never came back. Now at twenty-three, Keisha had experienced more drama in her short span than most women did in a lifetime. But, she refused to sit around and sulk about the hand that life had dealt her. She had Malik and Foster to think about, so she wasn't about to become the poster child for unwed black mothers. Instead, Keisha motivated herself to move on and be productive.

College was out of the question for the time being because that required paying a tuition, which Keisha could not afford. As an alternative, she took a training course at Brookdale Hospital and got a certificate as a home health aide with nursing assistant training. Keisha changed her identity by using the surname Blake when she entered the class. This way, she could work and still receive public assistance at the same time. The bank wouldn't accept Keisha's nametag as a form of ID to cash her paychecks, but she found a way to get around it. The owner of the liquor store in her neighborhood cashed checks for a small fee of five dollars, so Keisha went to him on payday, as did many other people.

Cece was released on parole after two years of good behavior by way of a women's halfway house program. While she was there, the directors assisted her in finding employment as a cleaning woman for an office building in Manhattan. Cece and Jahlil moved back in with Clara for the remainder of her parole period until she

151

got her own place out in Flatbush.

Keisha followed Cece's lead and moved into the same building. She and the boys had moved back in with her parents after Sonny got arrested because it was no longer safe for them to live in the building. The word on the street was that Keisha still had money from the bank robbery, which wasn't true because the Feds took it all when they trashed her apartment looking for it. But, as far as everybody else was concerned, Keisha was loaded, and the thugs on the block planned to rob her. When the word got back to Keisha, she packed up as much as she could, as fast as she could, and hauled ass.

T.J. fully reformed himself while paying his dues to society. He got his high school equivalency diploma and took up barbering as a trade. T.J. made sure to stay clear of Sonny's path while he was locked up, and with good reason. Sonny planned to have him dealt with, with no regards to him being Keisha's brother, because he had snitched on him.

T.J.'s snitch moniker didn't serve well on the block either, and many of the inmates sought after him. For protection, T.J. converted to the Nation of Islam. Thomas didn't share the same views of religion with T.J. because he followed the Christian faith, but he was proud of his son's achievements. Upon his release from Rikers Island, T.J. made it official and got his barbers license. Thomas gave him a chair at the barbershop.

Chapter 23

Baby Mama Drama

Five years later, during one of her many visits to see Sonny, Keisha ran into a young woman who was in her twenties. She was fair skinned, pretty, and curvaceous. The woman had traveled the same course as Keisha from the time they boarded the Manhattan bound train at Franklin Avenue, and she was now getting on the same bus. Since they were going in the same direction, Keisha sat next to her, and they struck up a conversation.

"Excuse me, I don't mean to be rude, but are you following me? It seems like you've been trailing me all day," Keisha stated humorously.

"Girl, I was about to ask you the same thing," the woman replied. She extended her hand to Keisha and introduced herself. "Hi, I'm Latoya. Nice to meet you."

"Hi, I'm Keisha, and likewise. I guess we're going the same way."

"We must be. This bus doesn't go but one way and back, unless you know something I don't," Latoya said.

"Not that I know of, but if you find out before I do, let me know because I could sure use a drink right now," Keisha answered. "I'm bringing a cooler with me for now on."

"I hear you. Let me guess. Your old man, right?" she asked.

"Yes. It's a surprise," Keisha answered. "He told me to take a break this week, but I know that he doesn't really mean it. He just hates that I have to travel so far."

"At least he's thoughtful," Latoya said. "My man made sure he got that collect call in to get them dollars dropped on his commissary. Didn't even bother to ask how his daughter was doing or nothing. Ain't that something?"

"Lucky you. I've always wanted a girl, but I do have two boys," Keisha stated.

"Don't worry; you'll pop one out sooner or later. Practice makes perfect," Latoya said while opening her purse and removing a photo from her wallet. "Here's my lil' mama. Her name is Sonya." She handed the photo to Keisha.

"Oh, she is so cute," Keisha commented. She then returned the photo to Latoya and asked, "How old is she?"

"Thank you. She'll be six in April," Latoya responded. "She's a handful, but I love her to death."

"I know what you mean. I have a nine-year-old and a seven-year-old. They really get on my nerves sometimes, but I wouldn't trade them for anything. Hold on a minute. I have pictures somewhere in here," Keisha said, searching through her purse. She presented two snapshots to Latoya. "The older one is Foster. That's my baby Malik in the other picture."

Latoya looked at the pictures. "They sure are handsome, but I would have sworn that the youngest boy was Sonya, if I didn't know any better. Look for yourself."

Keisha took the snapshots of both her son and Latoya's daughter and made a comparison to see if there was any truth to Latoya's theory. Latoya was correct. Malik and Sonya did favor each other.

"Oh my God, you're right, Latoya. They almost look like twins!" Keisha agreed.

"That's what I thought. I didn't notice at first, but then I

154

thought, 'Wait a minute. Is that my little boo-boo?'"

"I know, right? But, they say it's a small world. We could be related. Matter of fact, what's your last name?" Keisha asked.

"It's Pearson," Latoya replied. "What about you?"

"My last name is Johnson, but I never heard of any Pearsons being in our family tree. It must be a coincidence."

"I guess so. No Johnsons on my side."

When they arrived at the visiting center, Keisha and Latoya made plans to get up with each other after visiting hours so they could ride back together. Since Keisha had to use the restroom, Latoya went ahead. Minutes later, Keisha walked to the front desk to sign the visitor's sheet.

"Sonny Blake," she said, handing her ID to the deputy working the shift.

He was an elderly white man wearing thick glasses. His nametag read "Clark."

"You're just in time," he told her after retrieving Sonny's visitation list. "I just called him down for his first visitor. Sign here, and you can go right in," Clark said, handing Keisha the clipboard.

Keisha didn't pay much attention to what Clark said because he appeared to be senile and mumbled his words. However, as she read Sonny's visitation list, a blood racing spasm traveled through her body, which caused the hairs to stand on the back of her neck. The name "Latoya Pearson" was signed on Sonny's visitation sheet.

It all added up now. The nights Sonny came home late and lied about where he'd been, and the resemblance between Malik and Latoya's daughter. *This is why he didn't want me to come this week,* Keisha thought. It wasn't that he didn't want her to make the long trip. It was because he had put her off to see his other baby's mama instead. Keisha thought about the little girl's name. It was Sonya, and she was named after Sonny. Keisha felt like a fool. That was the first clue, but she didn't pick up on it. Then to add insult to injury, she had befriended the woman that Sonny was cheating with, and actually liked her.

Keisha walked towards the visiting room and stood in the doorway. Her eyes scanned the room like a radarscope. Finally, she spotted Sonny and Latoya sitting together at one of the tables in the middle of the room. Remaining calm, Keisha continued watching them to see how long it would take for Sonny to notice her. Eventually, he looked up with a startled expression on his face. That's when Keisha approached the table and stood over him.

"Surprise, baby," she said sarcastically.

Sonny didn't utter a word. He just sat with his head down and arms folded on the table.

Latoya was confused. While looking up at Keisha, she asked, "Keisha, how do you know my man, and why are you calling him baby?"

"Don't you get it, Latoya? He's been playing on us. Our kids are brother and sister. That's why they look so much alike. Right, Sonny?"

Latoya was heated. "Answer her, Sonny. Are you the father of her baby?" she asked, staring him down.

Sonny looked up at Latoya, dumbfounded now that he had been exposed.

"Yes, it's true. I'm Malik's father," he admitted. "And, Keisha, I have a little girl by Latoya, but I'm just finding this out," he added.

"You coward sonofabitch, how the fuck can you sit here and lie?" Latoya asked. "You're already busted, so at least tell the truth!"

Every person's attention in the visiting room was now focused on the drama act being displayed by Keisha, Sonny, and Latoya. One of the C.O.'s, a big thick-necked brother, came over when things started getting too loud.

"I'll have to escort you two off the premises if you don't keep it down," he said, addressing Keisha and Latoya.

"Don't bother. I'm leaving," Keisha replied and looked at Sonny. "I can't believe I was so blind, but now I know the truth," she said. "Sonny, I've been faithful to your trifling ass since day one, and for what? This bullshit? Well, take a good look. Because this is the last time you'll ever see my face up in this raggedy motherfucker. I hope you rot in this bitch!" She then looked at Latoya and said, "He's all yours."

The C.O. grabbed hold of Keisha's arm. "Ma'am, you'll have to come with me."

"Take your fucking hands off me! I know the way out!" Keisha said, pulling away.

Sonny called out to Keisha and tried to run after her, but the C.O. refrained him.

Keisha kept her word when she walked out on Sonny that day. She never returned to the correctional facility again, and thus, another relationship had ended.

Sonny tried calling Keisha collect, but she never accepted any of his calls. It got to the point where a collect call came from Rikers every day, until finally Keisha had to change her phone number all together. When Sonny discovered the number had been changed, he tried contacting her through the postal service. That is, when he had enough money on his commissary to buy an envelope and postage stamp. But, Keisha stayed firm in her conviction and tossed the letters out as soon as they arrived in the mail. However, she did send him pictures of Malik and had their son write something on the back. By doing so, Sonny got to see his son, and Malik could never accuse her of denying him of his father when he got older.

Chapter 24

Time is Money

K'shon cruised down Flatbush Avenue on gold rims, bumping the system in his black Cherokee Jeep SUV. Mounted on the dashboard was a plastic crown air freshener that had become the rave in automotive parts and accessories, and a pair of fuzzy dice dangled from the rearview mirror.

It was the spring of 1991. Crack, a freebase form of cocaine sold in small plastic vials, was the new drug on the streets, and it hit ghettos across the United States like a plague. A five- or ten-dollar hit seemingly became the solution to everyone's problems, but in actuality, it ruined families, lives, and communities as a whole. But, for dealers like K'shon, it was a "get rich quick" scheme, and he was on top of the game.

K'shon had a crackhouse in the Brownville Housing Projects and another one on Nostrand Avenue, where he was now headed. A great deal of K'shon's success resulted from the money he had stolen from Cece some eleven odd years ago. The same night he left her stranded in a cheap motel room as bait for the Feds. A narcissistic grin crept on K'shon's face while stares of envy emerged from the group of admirers that observed the ride as he rolled by. K'shon pulled up in front of Jahlil's building and saw him shooting craps. Jahlil greeted him as he got out of the car.

"Whaddup, K-Born," Jahlil said, extending his fist to get dapped.

"Yo, what I tell you about that, boy? I ain't with that five percent shit," K'shon snapped. "If that's what you about, then do you. But, when you address me, it's K'shon."

"My bad, man. I'm slipping," Jahlil responded.

"Yeah, you are slipping, lil' nigga. How the fuck you making my money when you're out here scratching for pennies? What, I ain't paying you good enough?"

At sixteen, Jahlil stood an even six feet tall and weighed a solid 170 pounds. He could have easily taken K'shon on, but he didn't mind being screamed on in public. K'shon paid him a handsome salary of five hundred dollars a week, which was more than the average adult could brag at the time. Jahlil had succumbed to the survival of the streets at age twelve. Cece, his mother, had also fallen victim to the lure of the vial-based poison, and they lived solely off of welfare. But, Cece disappeared when check day came around, so Jahlil learned to fend for himself.

For a hustle, he and his little homies would go into the supermarket and steal an economy-sized box of Pampers. Then, they'd slap a 'PAID' sticker on it, and sell it back to the store. As Jahlil got older, he upgraded to boosting designer clothes from department stores, and sold them at a fraction of the retail cost on the street.

At first, K'shon put Jahlil on as a lookout kid, and then later promoted him to a runner. When K'shon ran into Cece again, he gave her three grand as an apology, and Cece accepted the money with no grudge. In return, Cece let K'shon sell from her apartment for a small cut, but she never forgot how he got over on her.

"Nah, K'shon, I can't complain. You do look out for a nigga," Jahlil replied. "But, it ain't like I got shit to do right now. That's why I beeped you."

"Yeah, but when you out here bullshitting, that's bad for

business. You're still on the clock regardless. I'm docking you, too," K'shon barked.

"Damn! That's the second time this week," Jahlil complained. "My stack is gonna be short as fuck this week."

"And whose fault is that? Yours or mine?" K'shon asked. "You'll know better next time."

K'shon reached inside his Guess jacket, pulled out a package, and handed it to Jahlil.

"Run this up to the spot and chop it up. And don't waste any time 'cause—"

"Time is money," Jahlil interrupted, finishing K'shon's sentence.

*****

Cece met Jahlil downstairs before he could enter the building. She had waited all morning for K'shon to bring the package. Years of substance abuse had taken over Cece's appearance, and it showed on her face, too. The voluptuous body men once admired had now transformed into a dilapidated shell of a frame. During Cece's urgency to get her blast, she hadn't bothered to put on any clothing other than a green army fatigue jacket and a worn pair of pink house slippers.

"Jahlil, why didn't you let me know K'shon was here?" she said, as if she didn't know already. "What's good, K'shon," she asked, looking past Jahlil.

"Ain't shit, Cece. Business as usual," K'shon said. He couldn't believe how bad Cece looked since she'd become strung out over the rock. Nor could he believe this was the same bomb pussy that he wanted so badly back in the day. Now, he wouldn't touch her with a ten-foot pole.

What a damn waste. At least I got mine, he thought.

Cece turned her attention back to Jahlil. "Let me get something

161

to calm my nerves," she begged.

"Damn, Cece, let me get this shit upstairs first," Jahlil told her.

Cece had stopped acting like a parent when she started basing hard. So, Jahlil occasionally called her by her first name when he was upset, like he was at the moment.

"You better watch your mouth, young man. I'm the one who brought you into this world. Remember that!"

K'shon cut in. "Y'all need to take that personal shit upstairs, for real. And, Jahlil, don't forget what I told you."

"I know. Time is money. I got it," Jahlil answered.

"See, you're starting to learn, lil' nigga. That's good," K'shon said with cockiness.

He then walked back to the Jeep and got inside. The system blasted as he turned the key in the ignition.

"Y'all people have a wonderful day. I'm out," he said and drove off.

Once he got into the apartment, Jahlil threw the package on the kitchen table. Cece sat with him as he gradually started cutting up the eight balls that K'shon brought from the Brownsville spot. To Cece, it seemed as though Jahlil was taking forever to get the work finished. She tried to convince him into letting her have a rock.

"Jahlil, let me get a piece so I can run into the bedroom right quick," she said.

"You know you gotta wait until I get the count, Cece," Jahlil told her. "I already got docked twice for slipping this week. I don't wanna hear shit from K'shon about coming up short."

"Then let me help. You're taking too long, boy. I'm the one who showed you how to do it, remember?"

"If I were to let you get your hands on this, we'd both end up floating in the East River, just like Tiny. You know K'shon don't play when it comes to his money."

"K'shon did that to Tiny?" Cece asked.

"Yeah, it was him. I thought everybody knew that," Jahlil said.

"But, don't be bringing it up no more. Matter of fact, let's change the subject. These walls are thin."

"I can't argue with that, but hurry up with my shit, slow poke. I would've been had it done," Cece replied.

"Damn, Ma, stop being so greedy. I hate it when you get like this," Jahlil confessed. "Go in the bedroom or something. I'll call you when it's ready."

Cece got up from the table and went to stand in the doorway to her bedroom. "Jahlil, I know you're taller than me and you think you grown, but I'll still knock you on your ass. You better ask some damn body," she said, then slammed the door.

"Whatever," Jahlil replied as he continued working.

Jahlil hated seeing Cece in the condition she was in, and how the drugs had changed their lives for the worst. He remembered when he was younger and found a clear bag that was filled with some form of white powder resting in a sifter on Cece's dresser. When Jahlil asked Cece what was inside the bag, he was told it was foot powder. Jahlil knew he'd been lied to when Cece snorted a line of the substance and sent him out of the room so she could finish doing the rest of it. That was the beginning of Cece's downfall, the cocaine. However, back then, Cece still acted like a mother, Jahlil thought. She didn't represent the definition of the average mom, but that was never Cece's style. She was unique, and Jahlil understood that.

Jahlil wished there was some way he could get his mother back on the right track. Cece admitted herself into rehabilitation programs in the past on her own will, but she would only dry herself out for a few months and be back to the pipe. Jahlil felt responsible for his mother's addiction because he was supplying her habit. It wasn't his first choice, but he knew Cece would only cop from someone else who might possibly lace the drug with a more harmful substance. In any case, Cece was going to get high either way, but at least he knew where it was coming from.

When Jahlil finished packaging the product, he threw the stash into a brown paper bag and put it in the pocket of his windbreaker hoodie. Next, he went into his bedroom, grabbed his 9mm from under the mattress, and tucked it in his pants. He unlocked the door to go back out, but then he remembered Cece wanted her cut.

"Yo, Ma, I'm done!" he called out.

Still wearing the army jacket she had worn outside, Cece came running out of the bedroom.

"It's about time, boy. I thought I was gonna have to run up the street and ask Justice to let me hold something on credit, the way you was going," she said.

"Ma, I told you not to fuck wit' Justice no more. He into some foul shit. Plus, you don't know what you getting. You gonna fuck around one day and get caught out there. Keep on being hardheaded. You'll see," Jahlil stated firmly.

"Okay, Mr. Big. Since you're calling the shots, I won't go to Justice if that's what you want. But, tell me this. When I run out from now on, I won't get any long speech when I ask you for something, right?"

Becoming annoyed with Cece's greed, he came back inside and shut the door.

"See, this is what I'm talking about. I'm trying to tell you something for your own good, and you're negotiating. Why can't you just listen sometimes? You think I like seeing my own mama hooked on this shit? And look at the way you dress when you come outside. It's embarrassing. My boys be clowning me all the time 'cause you in the street begging when I'm not around. Then I gotta bust a nigga in his grill every time somebody says they saw my moms with a trick!"

Before he could get another word out, Cece slapped Jahlil across the face with a force that turned his head sideways. When his head came back straight, she slapped him once more for good measure.

Jahlil's eyes filled with rage as he stared Cece down. Had anyone else put their hands on him, he would have gladly pulled out his 9mm and blasted them on point. But, Cece was his mother, so she got away with it.

"Yo, what the hell you do that for?" he asked, rubbing his face.

"That's for being disrespectful," Cece answered. "How dare you stand there and judge me, like you're a saint!"

"I never claimed to be one, but I don't smoke. You do," he reminded her.

"No, you don't smoke, Jahlil. But, you're selling it, and that's just as bad," she fired back. "Just because you're wearing them high-priced clothes and got a little money in your pocket don't make you no better than me. All you do is jump for K'shon like a trained dog, and he don't give a damn about you. I hope you know that."

"What! K'shon is my peeps. If he ain't put me on, I'd probably still be out there on that weak hustle robbing department stores. Now, I'm paid."

"You know what, Jahlil? A hard head makes a soft ass. Keep on believing that shit, and it's gonna blow up in your face one day. And you can quote me on that."

"I am blowing up, 'cause I'm making mine," Jahlil said, beating his chest with enthusiasm. "I'll see you later. Your stuff is on the table."

After he left, Cece went to the table and looked at the clip that Jahlil had put together before he walked out. There were ten capsules. She reached into her coat pocket for her stem and a wire hanger. She pushed the pipe screen through the walls of the glass, then opened one of the capsules and packed the contents into the pipe. The hit was ready. Cece grabbed her cigarette lighter and flicked it, but Jahlil's voice reverberated in her head, haunting her. *But I don't smoke. You do.*

Guilt ran through Cece's conscience when she thought about

what her teenage son had said. The pipe had not only ruined her life, but his life, as well. As a mother, Cece's negligence pushed Jahlil away from her and into the hands of the wrong company. And since he was now footing all the household bills, including the rent, it seemed as if he didn't acknowledge her as a parent anymore. She was just another base head as far as he was concerned.

The awareness of shame sunk in, and Cece needed the comfort of the blaze to erase it. She put the pipe back to her lips and torched it. The combustion sizzled into a cloud of smoke as she inhaled. The buzz gave Cece's brain an intense stimulation and relaxed her mind, but not for long. To fill the void, she opened another capsule and continued to binge until the supply was gone.

*****

Downstairs, Jahlil sat on the front stoop with a fat, brown-skinned kid named Boot, whose real name was Devin. He once got stomped in a fight by a West Indian kid wearing black Timbs. The stamp on his forehead never went away, so the nickname stuck. Boot hung around Jahlil all the time, hoping K'shon would take interest and put him on as a worker, too.

It didn't take long for Jahlil to start pushing the product once he got outside. When the fiends saw him coming, they flocked to him like bees to a honeycomb. Within minutes, he had sold more than half the weight he was carrying. The other half was stashed in his mailbox for safekeeping in case the police showed up. It was a trick Jahlil had learned early in the game. He had seen too many young dudes get picked up for carrying the product on them, and he wasn't trying to get sent up for anyone, including K'shon.

The money was fast and easy, but Jahlil never understood why the customers stayed so loyal and gave up their hard earnings for a few pieces of crushed hope that was gone no sooner than they had bought it. Still, they kept coming back for more, and his pockets stayed fat. So, he didn't care.

With no one around except for Boot, Jahlil took the billfold from his pocket to count the profit he had made. Curious, Boot stood up and looked over Jahlil's shoulder. He tried to keep up with Jahlil's count as he flipped through the stack.

"Damn, son, that's a lot of loot. Looks like you got about half a G. Am I right?" he asked.

Jahlil elbowed Boot in the knee with all his might.

"Ouch! Why you do that?" Boot asked, rubbing his knee to relieve the pain.

"That was for being nosey. And stay the fuck from behind me, fat boy," Jahlil stated bluntly.

"Alright, man! You ain't have to hit me, though. I was trying to help you out. You know how we do. We got this shit on lock!"

"Nigga, *we* don't do a damn thing, and *I* got this shit on lock. I don't know why you be out here frontin' like you ballin'. You ain't puttin' in no work," Jahlil said.

"That's because you holding up the process," Boot replied. "I've been asking you to hook me up like forever. When are you gonna talk to the boss for me?"

"The boss? Nigga, are you listening to me? You don't work for nobody. I'll holler at K'shon when the time is right. Just stop jocking me, alright?"

"My bad. You still gonna look out for a nigga with that fiddy, right? I was kind of counting on it."

"Fiddy? Man, K'shon docked me, so I'm docking you, too," Jahlil said and handed Boot thirty dollars.

"Damn, you a coldhearted dude," Boot said, taking the money. "You're just gonna do your boy like that?"

"Business is business. You know the rules. Now get the fuck out of my face before I take it back," Jahlil replied.

Chapter 25

Boyz Will Be Boyz

Foster got off the B44 at the corner of Nostrand Avenue and Farragut Road rocking a red and white Nike tracksuit and a matching pair of Air Force Ones. Foster stood at a modest 5'8", but he was now taller than Keisha. He weighed 150 pounds of solid muscle and had the physique of a bodybuilder, all of which he acquired from weight training. Foster also inherited Detroit's good looks, and like his father, he had become quite the ladies' man. At age fifteen, he was already breaking the hearts of all the young girls in the neighborhood and dodging around corners to hide from the ones that chased him down. Foster and Detroit were like clones. The only thing that separated their DNA was Keisha's blood and his trademark cornrow braids.

He turned into the courtyard of the building, where Jahlil and Boot had just finished settling their financial dispute.

"Whaddup, 'Lil? Yo, Boot," he said, giving daps.

"What's good, Fist," Boot replied.

Fist was Foster's street tag because he was quick with his hands at boxing.

"Knowledge is born," Jahlil declared.

"Jahlil, don't play yourself, son. You know good and well you ain't a true god," Foster said.

"Ain't nobody playing, man. I'm true to this."

"So, if one of them came up to you right now and asked you today's mathematics, you would know it, right?" Foster asked.

"No, but that's only because I'm still studying. I did stop eating that swine, though."

"See, that's another lie," Foster stated. "You be swining and dining every day, and don't even know it."

"Nigga, you mad. When was the last time you saw me eating pork?"

"Remember last Sunday when my moms cooked them collard greens?"

"Hell yeah, I remember. Them shits was good as fuck," Jahlil responded, rubbing his stomach. "Aunt Keisha really knows how to throw down in the kitchen. I give her props."

"As a matter of fact, you had seconds, didn't you?" Foster asked.

"Shit, I think I ate like three plates."

"Well, I'm glad you enjoyed yourself, because they were seasoned with ham hocks," Foster said, laughing.

"Yo, that's fucked up! Why you ain't say nothing, man?"

"Please! Don't act like you didn't know. What the fuck did you think was in it, Adobo?"

"Damn, I need a laxative so I can cleanse my system out," Jahlil said.

Boot cut in on the joke. "Ha-ha! You're always talking about how I'm fronting, and look at you. Just wait until I tell everybody. They're gonna trip off of this!"

"You ain't gonna tell nobody shit, fat boy, unless you want me to pop a cap in your ass!" Jahlil said, lifting his windbreaker and exposing the 9mm.

Boot's face straightened up as he stepped back.

"Yo, cut him some slack, 'Lil. That shit was funny," Foster admitted.

"I'm just fucking with Boot. I ain't gonna hurt him," Jahlil said. "I know I'm not eating at your house anymore, though."

"We'll see about that tonight when your hungry ass comes banging on my door for another plate of food," Foster joked.

"And you know this!" Jahlil said, cracking up at Foster's remark.

Foster sat between Jahlil and Boot on the steps. "What were you guys getting into before I showed up?"

"Nothing much," Jahlil replied. "I just got through schooling this kid on the value of a dollar."

"You've got to be kidding me. Are you saying this big fool right here can't count?" Foster asked.

Boot jumped in. "Man, do you think I'm ignorant or something? I know how to count. We're talking about your man over here shortchanging people."

"You think I'm playing, don't you, Boot? Keep on talking, and see if I don't take that shit back," Jahlil threatened.

"Oh, y'all talking about that again," Foster said, catching on. "When are you guys gonna stop grinding for K'shon? Y'all making him rich while he's killing people off that shit."

Jahlil stood up and got in Foster's face. "Yo, son, I'ma tell you like this. Personally, I don't give a fuck about what a person does with their life, as long as I get mine. It's not like someone's forcing them to do it. They're doing it because they want to. It is what it is."

"True, but you're not getting the point," Foster replied. "The money looks good to you right now, but fast money isn't always good money. Can't you see what's happening? This shit out here is real. If you don't get out of the game now, one or two things are going to happen. One, you'll end up in jail, or two, you'll end up six feet under. If I were you, I'd leave that dude K'shon alone and get back in school."

"Well, you're not me, so mind your business," Jahlil said,

poking Foster in the chest. "School is not for everybody, and it's definitely not for me. I'ma get mine the best way I know how."

Foster let his school bag drop from his shoulder to the ground.

"Fuck you all up in my face for?" he said, shoving Jahlil. "You got me fucked up, but you ain't running shit this way!"

Jahlil turned his NY fitted to the side and grinned. "I'ma let that shit slide this time because you're like family. Next time, your ass is getting blasted. That's my word!"

Foster stepped even closer to Jahlil. "So you're gonna shoot me now? You ain't nothing but a punk. If you didn't have that gun, I'd split that fucking wig!"

"I'll be right back," Jahlil said before going into the building, where he went behind the staircase and stashed the 9mm in the mailbox. He returned pulling the windbreaker over his head and set it on the banister.

"I ain't got shit now, so what's up!" he said, getting in a fighting stance.

Foster stepped towards Jahlil. He had already taken off his jacket, contemplating that Jahlil was coming back to exchange blows. It was a common ritual they had practiced since they had gotten older. Jahlil was a year older than Foster, and he was also a lot taller. However, Foster possessed more strength, so they tested one another from time to time.

Foster immediately went in for the attack. He swung a right cross at Jahlil, but Jahlil blocked it and tagged Foster with a left jab to the chin, stunning him momentarily.

Foster brushed the hit off like it didn't faze him, when actually it did.

"Is that all you got, nigga? You hit like a bitch!" he said, shuffling on his feet like Ali.

"Yeah? We'll see about that after I knock your ass out!" Jahlil snapped.

Jahlil threw a wild haymaker, but Foster ducked and landed a

172

gut punch that knocked the wind out of him. By this time, a crowd had gathered. Some of the spectators instigated to keep the fight going.

"Oh snap! Did you see how shorty caught him? Look at dude's face. I think he just shitted on himself," one of them said.

"Damn, son, I know you ain't going out like that. Whip that ass," said another.

Jahlil looked around to see everyone was heckling him. He wasn't about to throw in the towel, but Foster's hands were too quick for Jahlil. Knowing that he would never defeat him toe to toe, Jahlil rushed Foster and tackled him to the ground. The crowd cheered on as the brawl altered into a wrestling match.

Keisha and Malik walked into the court. She had taken off earlier from work that day to attend a parent/teacher's conference at Malik's school. They had just come from the supermarket and were both carrying groceries. Malik, who stood five feet tall and weighed a mere ninety pounds soaking wet, dropped his bags and ran to his brother's aid as fast as his feet would take him.

"Yo, that's my brother!" he shouted and jumped on Jahlil like a wild cat.

Keisha pushed her way through the crowd to stop the fight.

"Boy, get your little behind up from there and pick up my groceries!" she said, pulling him off Jahlil. "And you two, stop it right now!" she added.

Foster and Jahlil obeyed Keisha's order and stopped fighting.

"Now, I want you both to explain what's going on here!"

"He started it first," Jahlil said.

"I did not. He's lying," responded Foster.

"Well, I'm going to finish it!" Keisha said and slapped them both upside the back of their heads. "Now, shake hands and call it a truce."

"Later for him! I'm not shaking hands with this fool!" Foster told her.

"And I'm not shaking his hand either!" Jahlil replied.

"Y'all think I'm playing? Neither one of you is too old for an ass whipping. Now, try me if you want and see what happens!"

Not wanting to be any more embarrassed than they already were, Foster and Jahlil complied with Keisha's demands and gave each other daps.

"Sorry, man. My fault," Jahlil admitted.

"It's all good. We fam," Foster replied.

"That's better. Now carry these heavy bags upstairs for me," Keisha said, then turned to the crowd behind her. "And take y'all nosey behinds home. This ain't pay-per-view!"

As Foster and Jahlil headed upstairs with the groceries, Boot stopped Keisha in the doorway, studying her from head to toe. Unlike Cece, Keisha had kept her appearance up. At thirty-four, she still made heads turn whenever she entered a room. Boot was one of her many admirers.

"Hello, Ms. Keisha. I must admit, you sure are looking extra lovely today."

"Thank you, Boot," Keisha replied and walked past him while thinking, *What the hell?*

Malik waited until Keisha reached the second floor landing before he stepped to Boot.

"What I tell you about looking at my mama, fat boy!" he said and punched Boot in the gut.

Boot keeled over in pain. When he finally straightened up, he saw Malik standing in the hall making funny faces through the window in the door. The door was locked, so Boot could not get to him.

Chapter 26

Skool Dazed

As a single parent, Keisha enforced strict rules upon her sons to keep them in line now that they were coming of age. It was a necessary effort since the streets were crawling with more than enough vices to easily lead them astray had she not. Keisha kept Foster and Malik busy by assigning household chores for them to do before they could go out, and on school nights, they had to be in the house before the streetlights came on. Along with keeping track of her sons whereabouts, Keisha also instilled in them the importance of education. Although the family was living comfortably off of her salary as a home health aide, Keisha always looked back and regretted the idea of dropping out of college. So, she expected more from her boys. Her tactics were effective, but no parent could keep up with a teenager twenty-four hours a day.

Deidra, a fourteen-year-old freshman, attended the same high school as Foster. Deidra had a pretty mocha complexion and curves like a grown woman. She had just moved from Queens to Brooklyn a few weeks ago, and she and Foster rode home on the same bus after school. Foster was already making plans to get acquainted with Deidra, but there was one problem—her girlfriends were always around. Foster knew he didn't stand a chance at getting close to Deidra with her friends present. More than likely, they would try and block him from getting to know her.

One day, Foster purposely missed his stop and stayed on the bus to see where Deidra was going. By doing so, he could at least find out where she lived and hopefully get her phone number in the process. That is, if he could ever get past her girlfriends. As it turned out, Deidra's friends got off the bus at Newkirk Avenue, which was only two stops away from where Foster lived. Most of the school kids were gone, with the bus now half empty. Deidra moved to the back and sat near an open window for fresh air. Seeing that this was his chance to move in on Deidra, Foster walked to the rear of the bus and sat directly across from her. Deidra looked up and smiled when she noticed Foster making his way towards her.

"I was wondering how long it was going to take you to say something. Were you scared?" she asked.

Foster was thrown off by Deidra's forwardness, but he didn't mind because it broke the ice.

"What are you talking about, girl? Ain't nobody scared. I was trying to holler at you earlier, but the bus was too crowded," he replied.

"So what are you saying then? You shy?"

"Nah, I ain't shy. I just don't like everybody being up in my business, nah mean?"

"Yes, I know what you mean, but why do you talk like that?" Deidra asked curiously.

"Like what?"

"Meaning, you don't pronounce all of the syllables in your words."

"'Cause that's the way I talk. Why? Something wrong with it?"

"No, I think it's kind of cute," Deidra said and giggled.

"That's what's up, but is that all you like?" Foster asked confidently.

"No. I think you have a nice body, too," Deidra answered

bashfully.

"Thanks. I work out." Foster flexed his biceps to impress her.

"Don't get suped, though," Deidra added.

"See, I was about to give you a compliment, but you're trying to dis' somebody. So, forget it now."

"Nobody's trying to dis' you, Foster. I'm just saying. As soon as I said you had a nice body, you started flexing like you were Mr. Olympia," Deidra commented, causing Foster to laugh.

"How'd you know my name?" he asked.

"Every girl at school knows who you are," she responded.

"That's all I ever hear. Foster this; Foster that. But, I bet you don't even know my name, do you?"

"I can't even front, because I don't know it," Foster admitted. "But, I'm waiting for you to tell me."

"My name is Deidra," she revealed. "Now what was the compliment?"

"Run that by me again?" Foster asked, unsure of what Deidra was saying.

"Before I told you my name, you said you were about to give me a compliment. What was it?"

"Oh, you mean that," Foster replied. "I was going to tell you that I thought you were cute, and I like you, too."

"Thank you," Deidra responded with a smile. "But was that it? I see how you be looking at me."

"So you peeped that, huh?" Foster asked, trying to get his swagger on.

"How could I not? You're so obvious with it. I think everyone notices when you stare. At least all of my friends do," Deidra answered.

"Well, from now on, I won't stare so hard. I wouldn't want to embarrass you in front of your girls."

"It's not embarrassing. I'm just letting you know that everybody can tell we like each other."

Yeah boy, I'm in there, Foster thought when Deidra openly confessed that she was attracted to him. However, Foster kept his cool and played it off like he was surprised.

"So that's why your friends be giggling and carrying on when I look at you? Y'all be talking about me?"

"Yeah, we do sometimes, but only when we catch you looking," Deidra confessed.

She peeped out the window and observed that Foster had gone way past his destination. She stuck her head back in and looked at him.

"Hey, why are you still on the bus?" she asked.

"Uh, because I'm going home," Foster replied, stretching the truth a bit.

"Don't lie to me, boy. You never come this far. Plus, I know you get off at Farragut Road," Deidra said, putting him on blast.

"Damn, girl, don't seem like nothing gets past you," Foster acknowledged.

"That's because I don't sleep on people, especially when I first meet them. My mama told me to always stay on my p's and q's. You'll never catch me slipping," she told him.

"I believe you. You know more about me than I do," Foster said. "I wouldn't be surprised if you knew my social security number."

"It's possible," Deidra replied wittingly.

She rang the bell to alert the driver that her stop was coming up. Foster followed her as she walked to the rear exit. Deidra stood in the steps of the door, but the bus driver saw her through the mirror and gave her a warning.

"No standing on the steps," he called out.

Deidra stepped back up on the landing to where Foster was standing behind her. The bus ran over a bump, and she lost her balance, stumbling into him. Foster caught Deidra by the waist to stop her from falling. She turned around to face him.

"Thank you," she said, gazing into his eyes.

"Don't mention it," he said modestly. "You a'ight?"

"Yes, I'm fine."

After the bus pulled up to the corner of Nostrand and Avenue D, they got off. School let out at 1:45 p.m. for Foster, and he normally got home between 2:15-2:20 p.m. Malik, on the other hand, was in the eighth grade and didn't get home until 3:40 p.m. Foster looked at his wrist and checked the time on his Casio G-Shock. It was 2:45 p.m. That gave him almost an hour to get home and let Malik in, so he saw no harm in offering to walk Deidra home.

"So how far do you live from here?" he asked.

"I only live two blocks up, but my mom is home by now," Deidra told him, but then thought for a second. "Hey, A Taste of Tropics is across the street. Let's stop and get a cone."

A Taste of Tropics was a West Indian based ice cream parlor in Flatbush, and it was more popular than 31 Flavors at the time. Foster hadn't gotten around to asking for Deidra's phone number, so he went along with the invite.

"That sounds cool. Let's go."

When they got inside, Deidra ordered a grape nut cone, which was her favorite, and talked Foster into having one, guaranteeing he would like it, too. They sat in a booth along the wall. Deidra took a big bite from her cone.

"Mmmm! I swear I can't live without this. I've got to have at least one of these a day."

"It is slamming," Foster agreed. "When you first said the name, I wasn't sure about trying it, but it's pretty good."

"Yeah, most people have that same reaction, but they change their minds right after they've tried one," Deidra confirmed, teasingly licking around the temple of the cone.

Her visual innuendo captured Foster's imagination, and his mind went completely in the gutter. In his mind, she was licking on something all right, but it wasn't an ice cream cone.

"See, you're doing it again," she said, breaking Foster's train of thought.

"Doing what?" he asked unknowingly.

"You're staring again."

"Yeah, but that's because you wanted me to. You know what you were doing," Foster declared.

"What was I doing, Foster? I'm just sitting here talking to you," she replied innocently, playing the dumb role.

"Don't even try to front, Deidra," Foster said. "I'm talking about the way your tongue went down on that cone. Nobody eats ice cream like that."

"Well, I do," Deidra boldly stated. She licked around the top of the cone and then stuck it in Foster's face. "Here, you want some?" she asked.

"Nah, that's a'ight. You probably put spit on it," he said, pushing Deidra's hand to the side.

"Oh, you got jokes now. See, you ain't even right." She giggled. "On the real, though, I asked you to come here so we could talk."

"That's cool as long as we ain't playing twenty questions," Foster said.

"It wouldn't be that many. Let's just talk," Deidra answered.

"Okay. So what do you wanna know?" Foster asked.

"Hmm, where should I start? I already know your name and where you live."

She thought about it and then came up with a solution. "I know. We'll do it like this. I'll ask you a question, and then you can ask me one. But you have to be honest. Bet?"

"Bet," Foster replied.

"Okay, I'll go first," Deidra said. "Do you have a girlfriend?"

"No," he answered.

"Stop lying, Foster. I see you with girls at school. You trying to tell me that you're not going out with any of them?" she asked.

"Just because you've seen me with a girl or two doesn't mean I'm going out with them. I have a lot of friends. And you asked two questions, so I go twice," Foster said.

"That sounds fair enough," Deidra agreed. "Okay, it's your turn. Ask me anything you want."

"A'ight then. How about you? Do you got a boyfriend?"

"No, I do not have a boyfriend," Deidra answered quickly. "Next question."

"Okay," Foster said. "Why haven't I seen you at school before until now?"

"I guess you weren't looking hard enough, because I've been there all the time," Deidra replied.

"Word. Then I must be slipping. I don't understand why I never saw you before."

"That's because I just moved here a couple of weeks ago," Deidra admitted and giggled.

"Don't laugh. I knew you was lying anyway," Foster said. "Ain't no way you could have snuck by me this long."

"And why is that, Foster?"

"Because I've got booty radar," he answered humorously.

"You stupid, I swear," Deidra remarked, laughing at him.

Foster saw he was scoring huge points with Deidra by applying his sense of humor, and that was good for the home team. But, he really wanted to learn more about her since they were hitting it off so well. Since Deidra was new meat at the school, he knew he had to act fast before someone else made a move on her.

"So where'd you move from?" he asked on a more serious note.

"We lived in Queens, but my parents divorced recently." Deidra confessed. "Daddy moved into the neighborhood with his new girlfriend, and my mom couldn't handle seeing them together. So, here we are."

"Wow, that was a punk move on your dad's part. How's your mom getting along now?" Foster asked with concern.

"She's coping better now," Deidra said. "Sometimes she cries in her bedroom when she's alone. I think that's the hardest part for her to deal with."

"Gee, I don't know what to say. I hate that for your moms, but at least she's making progress."

"Yeah, every day's a new challenge, but she's coming around. I just want my mom to be happy again. I hate seeing her this way," Deidra confessed.

"I feel you," Foster said. "But how are you coping? I mean, aren't you mad at him for leaving?"

Deidra grew silent as she stopped herself from becoming emotional. When her parents first separated, she despised her father with a passion for breaking up the family and deserting them. But, time heals old wounds, and he was still "daddy", so Deidra forgave him eventually.

"I was in the beginning, but then I realized my parents fought all the time. At least they get along now," she finally answered.

"That's one way of looking at it," Foster said.

"It's probably for the better anyway," she added before gobbling the last scoop of her cone. "Are your parents still together?"

Why did she have to go there? Foster thought. Sonny Blake was the only father he knew of, and he wasn't proud of that. He pretended not to hear her and toyed with his watch.

"Did you hear me? I just asked you a question."

Foster looked up. "Oh my bad, did you say something?"

"Yes, I did, and I know you heard me."

"I never knew my dad, so I don't talk about him. And moms is single," Foster told Deidra.

"I'm sorry. I didn't mean to pry. But if it made you uncomfortable to speak on it, that's all you had to say. You didn't have to ignore me," she replied.

"I wasn't igging you. I was checking the time."

"Whatever," Deidra said. "What time is it anyway?"

"Oh shit! It's three-thirty. I've got to get home!" Foster opened his Nike school bag and found a ballpoint pen. He then tore a sheet of paper from his notebook and gave it to Deidra. "Here, write your number down."

"Okay." She wrote her number down on the paper and handed it back to him.

"Is your mom okay with you talking to boys?" he asked.

"Yes, silly. Why wouldn't she be?"

"Hey, some parents are strict," he answered from experience.

"I can have friends, but I'm not allowed to date until I'm sixteen."

"That's cool. We just won't tell her," Foster joked.

"You're funny," Deidra said as they walked out the door.

They stopped and faced each other when they got to the corner.

"Well, I guess I'll see you tomorrow at school," she said.

"Can I call you later?" he asked.

"You have my number, don't you?"

"A'ight, bet." Foster leaned over slightly to kiss Deidra on the cheek, but she surprisingly parted her lips and gave him a French kiss. It was brief, but Foster didn't complain.

"See you later," Deidra said and strutted off. She swayed her hips teasingly with each step, knowing that Foster was watching.

"Later," Foster answered with his eyes glued on Deidra's butt. *Damn her ass is fat*, he thought.

Foster crossed the street and waited at the bus stop. He checked the bus schedule mounted on a pole at the corner for the next arrival. Suddenly, three Trini youths appeared out of nowhere. One of them approached Foster. He was a slim kid and sported long dreadlocks that were tucked inside a Rasta-styled knit cap.

"A, bwoy, wey yuh a look pon?" he asked.

183

"Come again?" Foster replied unknowingly.

"Yuh nuh ovastan?"

"Look, man, either you speak in English or leave me the fuck alone," Foster said.

"'Dis battie think 'im a rude bwoy!" a second kid said, as his friends snickered at the joke.

"Yo, fuck you, punk!" Foster retaliated.

"Mi a mash up yu Ras clot, bwoy!" the second kid said, stepping to Foster.

The three youths now had Foster surrounded. Not being one to back down from a fight, Foster dropped his bag and prepared for battle. Just then, a familiar voice echoed from the street intersection.

"Yo, what the fuck is going on!" Jahlil shouted, stepping out of a '84 Nissan 300 ZX. Boot was behind the wheel. He parked the car on the corner beside the bus stop and jumped out.

Jahlil stood at Foster's side. "What's up, son? You got beef?" he asked, with his hand on the 9mm that was tucked in his waist.

"I don't know. Ask them," Foster said, now relieved that the odds were even.

Jahlil turned to the kid with the dreads. "So what's up? Do we have a problem?"

"Yo, bredda, everything is irie. Sekkle," he replied calmly after seeing Jahlil's hand on the burner.

"Then step now!" Boot stated bravely in a fake Trini accent of his own.

"Cool runnings," answered the kid with the dreads. "A'right, leggo," he told his friends.

"Yeh, mon," one of them agreed, and they departed.

Boot, Foster, and Jahlil hopped back in the car and headed home. On the way, they recapped Foster's run-in with the Trini youths.

"Yo, did you see how fast they moved when I told them to step?" Boot asked.

184

"Yeah, Boot, you really scared them off. I suppose this gat I'm carrying had nothing to do with it," Jahlil stated sarcastically.

"Boot was popping mad shit," Foster added. "I never saw this kid get up that much heart before."

"We had your back, son," Boot boasted. "You're lucky we came when we did. Them yard boys was about to put that capoeira on your ass. You would have been hurt."

"Nah, Boot, I wasn't getting caught with no flying kicks like you did," Foster replied. "But, I was glad when y'all came through."

"What are you doing around here anyway?" Jahlil asked.

"I met this shawty on the bus. I was just making sure she got home," Foster replied.

"Well, I hope she was worth it, kid. You almost got the beat down of a lifetime behind that shit," Jahlil remarked.

"Trust me, she's thorough," Foster assured him. "What y'all doing riding around in Boot's mom's car?"

"Oh, we just came from the Brownsville spot," Jahlil told him. "K'shon put Boot on to do pickups since he got the permit. He says it'll save him time from traveling back and forth."

"That's right," Boot said. "I'ma be ballin', son!"

"Just be careful, man," Foster warned him.

When they got back around the way, Boot let Foster out in front of the building.

"Yo, kid, we gotta make this run for K'shon. Catch you later," Jahlil said.

"A'ight, man, and thanks for looking out," Foster said and walked into the courtyard.

"Stay away from Avenue D, son. It's bad for your health!" Boot joked before pulling off.

Malik was sitting by himself on the stoop reading a comic. It was after 4:00 p.m., and he was hot.

"Took you long enough," he emphasized, pointing to an

imaginary watch on his wrist.

"Sorry about that, lil' brother," Foster said apologetically. "How long you been waiting?"

"Man, don't try to play me like that. You know what time it is," Malik cried. "And where were you? You made me miss Video Music Box."

"I had to stop at the library to get a book for a school assignment."

"Why you lying? The library's up the street. I just saw you get out the car with Boot and 'em. I'ma tell Mommy how you had me waiting out here when she gets home."

"Yo, come on, Malik. Why you always gotta be a little bitch?"

"Now I'm definitely telling her!" Malik promised.

"Wait a minute, Malik," Foster said, going into his pocket. He dug out a crumpled one-dollar bill. "Take this. You can go play a few games of Pac-Man at the pizza shop."

"Give me another one, and it's a deal," Malik bargained.

Foster searched his pockets once again and scraped up seventy-five cents.

"Here, this is all I got, you little crook." He dumped the change into Malik's hands. "And you better get back here before Mommy gets home."

"Thanks, Foster," Malik said and went about his business.

Chapter 27

Cold Feet

Foster went up to the apartment and did his homework. When he finished, he did his workout routine and showered. A few hours had passed since he'd left Deidra at the bus stop, and he was anxious to give her a call. He had placed Deidra's number on the top of the dresser in his bedroom, but when he went for it, it was gone. He searched frantically through his Nike school bag to see if it was in there, but it wasn't. Foster walked to the closet to go through the pockets of the clothes he had worn earlier that day, when he noticed Malik sitting on the bed with a sheet of notebook paper in his hand. Malik jumped and hid the note behind his back when he felt Foster's presence in the room.

"Hand it over, Malik," Foster demanded.

"What?" Malik asked innocently.

"Don't play with me. You know what I'm talking about."

"I ain't got nothing, man. Leave me alone."

"So what are you hiding behind your back then?"

"Don't worry about it. It ain't yours."

"I left a note on the dresser, and I know you got it, Malik!"

"Man, I told you I ain't got nothing. Now get out my face!" Malik said, sticking to his word.

Foster started to lose patience with his younger brother. "I'm counting to three, Malik. That note better be in my hand, or I'm fucking you up!" he threatened.

"You better not touch me, Foster," Malik said, now frightened.

"One…"

"I'm serious. Leave me alone!"

"Two…"

"Get away from me!"

"Three!"

"Mama!" Malik yelled at the top of his lungs.

Foster tried to pry the note from Malik's hand, but Malik held on tightly and wouldn't let go. Keisha rushed in the room when she heard the commotion. She grabbed Foster from behind and pulled him off Malik. Malik got up and ran behind Keisha, using her as a shield between himself and Foster.

"What I tell you about putting your hands on your brother?" she asked Foster, while Malik taunted him from the rear.

"Why you taking up for him? He started it," Foster told her. "And he's laughing at me. Look at him!"

Keisha looked down at her side and saw Malik smiling.

"You find something funny, Malik?" she asked.

"No, ma'am."

"Bring your butt around here so I can see your face!" she stated firmly.

"Yes, ma'am," Malik answered and came from behind her. He stood between Keisha and Foster.

"Now what's the problem? I heard you two from the kitchen."

"Foster came in here and hit me for nothing, Mommy."

"He's lying, Ma," said Foster defensively. "I was trying to get a note he took from the dresser, but he wouldn't give it back."

Keisha looked Malik straight in the eyes. "Is this true, Malik?" she asked.

"Yes, ma'am, but I didn't know it was his when I picked it up," he replied guiltlessly, even though he'd been caught.

"I should slap the mess out of you for lying to me, boy. Hand it over!" Keisha said with authority and confiscated the note.

"Can I have that, please?" Foster asked, not wanting Keisha in his business.

"I'll give it to you in a minute. Just wait," she replied.

"But, Ma, you're invading my privacy," he countered.

"Boy, I'm the one paying the bills up in here. As long as you live under my roof, you don't have any privacy. Understand?"

"Yes, ma'am," Foster answered.

Keisha opened the note and looked at it. The name *Deidra* was underlined with a number written below.

"Is this what all the fuss is about, a phone number?"

"Foster has a girlfriend. That's why he was mad," Malik said.

"Mind your business before I punch you!" Foster stated angrily.

"Don't press your luck, Foster. I just warned you about that," Keisha said boldly.

"Why you getting on me and not him? You see he keeps starting with me," Foster retaliated.

"Oh, don't think Malik's in the clear," Keisha said. She turned to Malik. "You go into my bedroom and wait for me to decide your punishment."

"Can I stay in here, please? I'll be quiet."

"Did you not hear what I just said?" she asked, now heated by Malik's annoyance.

"Yes, ma'am, but your room's full of perfume bottles. The smell is gonna give me a headache."

"You're gonna have an ass ache if you don't get out of here, boy!" Keisha promised.

"Aaaaah...you played yourself, son!" Foster said, instigating the situation.

"Foster, mind your business or you'll be next," Keisha said. "Now get out of here, Malik," she added.

Foster was relieved when Malik finally left the room. The quarrel was getting intense, and he was afraid Malik would snitch on him about coming home late. He could have told that Malik was at the pizza shop playing video games on a school day, but he was the one who had encouraged him to go. So, Keisha would have grounded them both.

Keisha turned her attention back to Foster. "Now, who is this Deidra girl," she asked curiously.

"Why is everybody so nosey today? First, Malik is all in the Kool-Aid, and now you."

"I'm your mother. I'm supposed be nosey," Keisha replied. "Now back to the question. Who is this Deidra person that's got you acting all hostile, and how long have you been dating her?"

Foster blushed at Keisha's allegation. "I'm not dating her, Ma. She's just a girl that goes to my school."

"A lot of girls go to that school, but this one's got you sprung," Keisha pointed out.

"Sprung? Ma, I ain't sprung over no girl. I kicked it to her on the bus and got the digits, that's all."

"So it's like that, Foster? You kicking it now?" Keisha asked teasingly, which made Foster blush again.

"C'mon, Ma, why you keep messing with me?"

"I'm not messing with you, player. You the one who got the… what's that word you said…designs?"

"What?" Foster asked.

"The girl's phone number," Keisha said.

"Ma, it's not designs. It's digits. And please don't say that in public. People might think you're retarded," Foster replied jokingly.

"You know what I meant," Keisha said, laughing at herself.

Keisha looked at Foster for a second and realized her son was becoming a young man. He was at the age where boys became seriously interested in girls, and it was only natural that sexual curiosity would soon come into play. That's if he wasn't already sexually active, but Keisha truly doubted he was. Nevertheless, Keisha felt it was time she and Foster had a heart to heart talk about the facts of life before it was too late.

"Foster, I'm going to ask you a question, and I want you to tell me the truth," she said on a serious note.

"Okay...shoot," he replied.

"I want to know if you're still a virgin."

Keisha's question caught Foster by surprise, and he thought she was way out of line for asking. Truthfully speaking, he was a virgin. However, sex wasn't a topic he wanted to discuss with his mother. In fact, the mere thought of it grossed him out. In any matter, he was going to find a way to change the subject.

"It was nice talking to you, Ma," he said while physically guiding Keisha towards the bedroom door to see her out.

"Hold on, boy. I'm not done with you yet," Keisha said.

She did an about-turn and walked back in the room.

"Why are you trying to get rid of me, Foster? You got something to hide?" she asked with suspicion.

"I ain't got nothing to hide, Ma. I just don't feel comfortable talking to you about sex," he replied.

"And why not? We talk all the time." Keisha grew more curious to know why Foster was evading the question.

"Yeah, but not about sex," he answered. "That's just something a guy doesn't discuss with his mom."

"I understand where you're coming from, but this is serious," Keisha told him. "You're too young to be a parent, and I'm definitely not ready to be anybody's grandmother."

"I'm not getting the point. All of this over a phone number?"

Foster asked. He really didn't understand why Keisha insisted on continuing with the conversation.

"Don't most relationships start with a phone number and a date? I'm sure that's the reason you asked that girl for her number, isn't it?"

"I guess so," Foster admitted.

"Then don't stand there and act like you don't know what I'm talking about. Now, are you a virgin or not?" she asked again.

Keisha's persistence was starting to wear Foster down. He was tired of going back and forth with her, so he answered truthfully.

"Yes, I'm a virgin, Ma," he shamefully confessed. "Are you happy now?"

"Is that the truth?" Keisha asked.

"Yes, it's the truth."

"Then I'm ecstatic," she said, grinning from ear to ear.

"Now I wish I would have lied to you. It would have been less embarrassing."

"Why? There's nothing to be ashamed of. You should be proud of your virginity. Trust me, when you get older, you'll look back and be happy that you waited for the right girl to come along," Keisha said inspiringly.

"Thanks for trying to make me feel better, but it's not working," Foster responded humorously. "Now can I go so I can make this call?"

"Yes, but don't be on the phone too long. I'm expecting a call from Mama. Your stubborn grandfather hasn't been taking his insulin, and your grandmother just took him to the emergency room."

"Is Gramps gonna be alright?"

"He will be once he gets the proper care he needs."

"Cool," Foster replied. "Oh well, let me make this call real quick."

"And make sure you answer if someone beeps in," Keisha reminded him.

"I will," he promised.

Foster left the room and went to use the telephone that was in the kitchen. He'd have rather used the phone in Keisha's bedroom for more privacy, but her room was off limits, with the exception of Malik who was now awaiting punishment. Foster dialed Deidra's number and waited. She picked up after several rings.

"Hello," she said.

"Hi, may I speak to Deidra please?"

"Speaking. Who is this?"

"Whaddup, girl? It's Foster," he said in playa mode.

"Hey, what's up. I was just thinking about you," replied Deidra.

"For real?" he asked.

"Yes. I had fun kicking it with you at the ice cream parlor today. I wish we could have stayed longer," Deidra admitted.

"Yeah, that was cool," Foster answered, not mentioning his run-in with the Trini youths. "Your moms must be sleeping, though," he added.

"Why you say that?" Deidra asked.

"Because you all loud wit' it. I know she ain't around."

"Nah, my mama's at work. She won't be home until midnight," Deidra replied. "Hold on a minute."

"A'ight," Foster said as she stepped away.

Foster kept the phone to his ear and waited for her to come back. As he listened, he heard a loud thump followed by a series of cuss words. Deidra returned to the phone shortly after.

"Sorry I took so long. I was in the shower when you called. I had to turn it off."

"No problem," Foster said. "What was that noise, though?"

"What noise?" Deidra asked.

"It sounded like an earthquake," he replied.

"Oh no! You heard that? How embarrassing," Deidra said and started laughing. "I fell when I ran into the bathroom. The floor was wet, and I'm only wearing a towel."

"Dayumn, I know you hurt. That shit was loud," Foster said jokingly. "You a'ight, though?"

"Yeah, I'm good. My butt just sore."

Foster was about to speak, when another call beeped in.

"Is that your phone or mine?" Deidra asked.

"It's probably for my moms. She's expecting a call," Foster told her. "Let me call you back."

"Okay," Deidra said and hung up.

The call was from Victoria. As it turns out, Thomas hadn't taken his medication longer than he admitted, so he was kept in the hospital. Since T.J. had a family of his own now and had moved out several years ago, Victoria would be left alone. Keisha packed an overnight bag and went to spend the night with her mother to keep her company. She clarified a few ground rules with Foster and Malik before she left.

"Okay, you guys. Dinner is on the stove, and I want you both in bed at a decent hour. And, Malik, you know your brother is in charge. So, you listen to him. And don't be picking on him, Foster."

"Mommy, can I come with you? I wanna see Gramps?" Malik asked.

"Malik, you have school in the morning. You know that. We can all visit Grandpa and Grandma tomorrow when I get off work, okay?" Keisha promised.

"Okay," Malik responded.

Within the next minute, T.J. pulled up to take Keisha to their parents' house. He beeped the car horn to let Keisha know he was outside.

"Alright, you two, I'll see you tomorrow afternoon, and behave yourselves." Keisha kissed them both and walked out the door.

It was well after nine o'clock at night. The door to the building stayed lock, so no one could enter unless they had a key or got buzzed in. But, there was always a crackhead or two that snuck in behind somebody coming or going so they could smoke on the roof. Foster went into the living room and looked out the window to see that Keisha got in the car safely. When he saw she had, he fixed Malik's dinner plate and made him go to bed afterwards. He waited until Malik was fast asleep before calling Deidra back.

"Hello," she said, answering.

"What's up? It's me again. Did I wake you?" Foster asked.

"Nah, you good, I always wait up for my mom to get home before I go to bed. I guess it's a habit."

"So what do you do while your moms is working? That's a long time to be waiting."

"Well, after my homework is done, I watch TV, but it gets boring after a while. I hate being here by myself. When it gets late, I hear strange noises, and they scare me," Deidra confessed.

Deidra revealed a vulnerability that Foster was aware of. Like most teenage girls, or even most women for that matter, she was afraid of being in the house by herself. This was Foster's chance to ask Deidra if he could come over. Her mom wouldn't be home for hours, and Keisha was gone for the whole night. The question was whether Deidra would go for it or not. Foster eased his way into asking her.

"Damn, it's a shame you're all alone. I wish I could be there so you wouldn't have to be afraid," he cleverly hinted.

"I would like that, but my mom gets home in less than three hours. I wish you could, though," Deidra replied.

"I'll be gone way before then," Foster said. "I can leave at eleven o'clock. I just wanna see you again."

"I would let you come over, but you can't take the bus. It'll take forever. My mom would be home by the time you got here," said Deidra.

"Then I won't take the bus. I'll call a cab," Foster told her.

"Alright, I guess, but you have to leave at eleven o'clock exactly," instructed Deidra.

She told Foster the address, and he wrote it down.

"No problem. I'll see you in about fifteen minutes, a'ight?"

"Okay, but hurry up," Deidra replied, then hung up.

Foster went into his closet and grabbed a dark hoodie and a pair of matching jeans that would blend in with the night sky since he was going into another neighborhood. He made sure Malik was asleep before he quietly tipped out the door and locked it.

Once outside, Foster ran to the corner and immediately hailed a dollar cab. He gave the driver the directions, and he took off. On the way, Foster remembered Deidra mentioning she was wearing nothing but a towel when he first called, and he hoped she was still in it when he got there.

Deidra lived in an apartment building on East 93rd and Kings Highway. Foster got out of the cab and walked into the lobby. He rang the intercom when he found Deidra's apartment listing.

Hearing the intercom, Deidra ran to the door. "Who is it?" she asked with caution.

"Foster," he replied, and she buzzed him in.

Foster searched each apartment door looking for 1-E. A soft voice echoed throughout the hall not far from his position. Foster lifted his head and saw Deidra standing in her doorway. She was no longer in a towel as he had hoped, but she was wearing an eye-popping sleepwear set with short-fitting bottoms that revealed her provocative young curves.

"Pssst...over here," she whispered, while drawing him near with her fingers.

Foster took his time getting to Deidra, and the delay annoyed her. When he reached Deidra, she grabbed him by the nape and pulled him inside. She locked the door and turned around. Foster could tell she was upset by the look on her face. He was about to ask what was wrong, when Deidra gave him a stiff shot to the arm.

"Hey! What was that for?" he asked, rubbing where she had hit him.

"Give me your shoes. You can't wear them in here."

Foster did as he was told and gave Deidra his Timbs. She put them in the closet by the foyer.

"That's for being so slow," Deidra finally answered. "I'm steady telling you to c'mon, and you taking your time like we got all night. My neighbors could have seen you, boy."

"My bad. I wasn't thinking. You forgive me?" Foster asked.

He walked up to Deidra and grabbed her by the waist. He kissed her on the neck while asking for forgiveness.

"You're lucky. I wasn't gonna let you in," Deidra replied, giving into his touch.

She took Foster by the hand and led him to her bedroom. She shut the door when they stepped inside.

Taking this as a hint, Foster kept the momentum going. Foster sat down on Deidra's bed that was near the window and pulled her atop as he laid back. Their eyes locked as Deidra inched her head towards his. She kissed Foster twice on the lips before pushing her tongue in his mouth. Foster put his arms around Deidra and rested his hands on her bottom.

When Deidra didn't complain, he eased his fingers under her shorts and thirstily groped her buttocks. The scent of teenage lust filled the air, and Foster acquired an erection. When Deidra felt the swell of his muscle poking her in the stomach, she sat up and smiled.

"You like my ass, don't you?" she asked, while stroking

197

Foster's hardened penis through the fabric of his jeans.

"No doubt," he answered.

"Damn, you hard as fuck. I wanna see it," she said.

"Then go for yours," he responded bluntly.

Deidra unfastened Foster's belt buckle and unzipped his jeans. She reached inside his boxers and pulled out his manhood, holding it in the palm of her hand and studying it with fascination.

"It's not moving," she said, now looking at Foster.

"It isn't moving because it's hard right now," he replied, shaking his head.

The sound of footsteps entering the apartment came from the front door. Foster and Deidra were so caught up in each other that they didn't hear when Deidra's mother came in.

"Shhh, be quiet. It's my mom," Deidra said, panicking.

"I thought you said she didn't get home until twelve?" Foster whispered.

"She must have got off early," Deidra responded. She shoved Foster aside and opened the window. "Sorry, but you gots to go. My mom will kill me if she finds you in here."

"What about my Timbs?" Foster asked.

"I'll bring them to school tomorrow. Now go," she ordered.

The footsteps came closer. Foster climbed through the window and got out just before Deidra's mother walked in the room. Deidra drew the curtains together.

"What are you doing, child?" her mother asked.

"Oh, hi, Mom. It was warm in here, so I opened the window," she answered.

"Girl, shut that window and go to bed," her mother replied.

"Yes, ma'am," Deidra said, relieved she didn't get caught.

Deidra's window led to an alleyway fenced with a gate and aligned with barbwire. Foster took a milk crate and stacked it onto a trashcan for leverage. He climbed up and took a deep breath. He paced his timing and hopped over the fence with the grace of a cheetah, but his hoodie got snagged on the barbwire. Foster was now suspended in midair, hanging on the other side of the fence. He tried to pull himself down, but that didn't work. So, he slipped out of the hoodie and crashed to the ground. Foster got up in pain. His jeans were torn at the knee, and he had twisted his ankle when he landed. He snatched the hoodie from the fence and limped away.

Foster walked for blocks before he came to a payphone. He hit Jahlil's pager with a 911 code so he'd know it was an emergency. Jahlil called back within five minutes. Foster answered the call immediately when the phone rang.

"Yo, 'Lil," Foster said anxiously.

"Who this?" Jahlil asked.

"It's me...Foster. You with Boot?"

"Yeah, he's right here. Whaddup?"

"Nothing. I just need a ride."

"Yo, where you at?"

"I'm on East 98th and Kings Highway."

"What the fuck! You ain't learn shit from earlier, did you?"

"Man, stop bullshitting and hurry up."

"Okay, man, hold tight. We'll be there in a few."

"A'ight. One."

"One."

Boot and Jahlil got to Foster within ten minutes. Boot had parked across the street from the payphone. He did a U-turn and came around when he saw that Foster was standing in his tube socks.

"Damn, they jacked you for your kicks? That's fucked up, dude," Boot commented.

"Man, ain't nobody jack me for shit. I was at Deidra's crib," Foster said while getting in the car.

"So where the fuck are your shoes?" Jahlil inquired.

"Her moms was at work, but she came home early. I had to climb out the window," Foster confessed.

"Did her moms see you?" Jahlil asked.

"I don't think so. I was ghost by the time she came in the bedroom," Foster replied.

"This kinda shit only happens to you, nigga," Jahlil commented, shaking his head. "At least tell me you got the pussy."

"No, but I was about to when ma'dukes showed up."

"Damn, you went through all that trouble and still ain't hit the pussy? Nigga, you ain't ever gonna hear the end of this," Jahlil declared.

"Word," Boot added.

"Man, fuck y'all. Just take me home," Foster said, and they drove off.

Chapter 28

Best Friends Forever

Keisha got off work and stopped at the corner store on her way in. She needed side dishes to go with the pork chops she was preparing for dinner. Fridays normally meant potluck night for everybody, but since Keisha had an easy day at work, she decided she'd cook tonight.

When she left the store and walked into the building's courtyard, she saw Cece standing in the hall and peeping through the glass window in the door. Cece let Keisha in when she saw her coming.

"Hey, girl, long time no see," she said casually.

Keisha took a long look at her childhood friend. She couldn't believe how bad Cece had let herself go. She was wearing an old tattered house robe, and a scarf was secured around her head to cover her damaged perm. She and Keisha weren't as close as they used to be. They became distant over the past two years when Cece started basing, but they were on speaking terms. Cece came by to see Keisha on occasions, but the visits normally ended with her borrowing money to get high, and Keisha was tired of supporting her habit.

"Hey, Cece. It has been a long time," Keisha said. "How have you been?"

"I'm hanging in there," Cece replied modestly. "Are you just getting in?"

"Yeah. I had to stop and pick up a few things at the store, but I'm finally home for the weekend, thank God."

"I know that's right," Cece responded.

"Do you mind helping me upstairs with the bags? I tried calling the boys earlier, but the phone was busy."

"I got you, girl," Cece said, taking one of the bags.

Keisha called for Foster and Malik when they got inside in the apartment.

"Foster and Malik, come put these groceries away," she yelled.

She and Cece both sat at the kitchen table. Keisha kicked out of her shoes.

"Oh, my poor feet," she said, rubbing the bottom of her heel.

"You better soak those puppies in some Epsom salt. I know them heavy-ass Dutch shoes be killing your feet. They look like they weigh a ton," Cece joked, referring to Keisha's nursing shoes.

"You ain't lying about that," Keisha said with a slight laugh. "They go with the uniform, though. So, I have no choice but to wear them."

"Yeah, but why you buy them so thick? They remind me of the platform shoes people used to wear back in the seventies."

"I bought what the store had, Cece. I didn't have time to go window shopping," Keisha said, now massaging her other foot.

"That's what you get for shopping at Florsheim. They don't sell nothing but Medicaid shoes."

"Forget you, Cece. But, I might have to slip some Dr. Scholl's inside these bad boys the way my feet be hurting."

Malik came running after he put his video game on pause. "Hi, Mommy," he said, squeezing Keisha with a big hug.

"Hey, baby," Keisha replied and returned the embrace.

"Hey, little man," Cece interrupted. "You don't see me sitting here?"

"Oh, hey Aunt Cece," he answered.

"Where's your brother? I called the house about an hour ago, but the line was busy. Who was on the phone?" Keisha asked.

"It was Foster's job. They called and asked him to come in," Malik answered.

"But he only works on weekends. Why did they call him in on a Friday? They know that boy is still in school."

"I guess the store was busy, Mommy."

"Foster's working now?" Cece asked.

"Yeah, he went and got himself a part-time job. He's a stock boy at Royal Farms," Keisha answered.

"Well, go 'head, Foster," Cece said. "I am surprised, though, Keisha. You hardly let them boys out of your sight."

"That is true, Cece, but Foster has expensive taste. I'm not buying all the things he asks for. I told him he could wear one-hundred-dollar tennis shoes as long as he's paying for them."

"I know that's right," Cece agreed. "Who's keeping an eye on Malik?"

"Foster's with him until he leaves out, but Malik can pretty much fend for himself now. If he gets hungry, he'll throw a Pop-tart in the microwave and grab a glass of milk until I get home."

Cece looked at Malik. "So you grown now, huh?"

"Nope, I'm just getting bigger," he answered. "I'll be taller than both of you by the end of the summer," he said confidently.

"I bet you will," Cece said to build his hope.

Malik had an inferiority complex. He was undersized in both height and weight, and it bothered him.

"Tell Aunt Cece what you told me yesterday, Malik," Keisha said.

"I'm going to be a superstar in the NBA just like Jordan," Malik boasted.

"That's right, baby. Go for that big money," Cece said encouragingly.

"Yep, I'ma be rich!" he added.

"Don't you forget about us po' folks when you become a big star."

"I won't," Malik promised. "When I get rich, I'm buying Mommy a big house in California, and you can visit us all the time!"

"Why I gotta visit? Don't I get a big house? I wanna rub elbows with the celebrities, too," Cece said humorously.

"Okay, Aunt Cece. I'll buy you a house right next to Mommy. Then you can keep her company when I go on the road."

"Aw, bless your heart. I'ma hold you to that promise, too, lil' man."

"That's my baby," Keisha said, squeezing him tightly. "Now how about putting these groceries away before the draft picks."

"Yes, ma'am," Malik responded and then did as he was told.

"So how was school today?" Keisha asked as he worked.

"It was alright until Mr. Hirsch gave us that pop quiz at the end of the day."

"And who is Mr. Hirsch?"

"He's my science teacher, Mommy. You met him when you came up to my school, remember?"

"I believe you, but I can't remember the names of all your teachers."

"Well, I hate him, and I hate pop quizzes," Malik confided. "He should have told us first so we could have studied."

"That's the purpose of a pop quiz, Malik. It wouldn't be a surprise if he told you. That's why I tell your butt to pay attention in class."

"I do pay attention in class. I'm not like the other kids who goof off all day."

"I'm glad to hear you say that, Malik, 'cause you know I don't play when it comes to your grades," Keisha said. "So how did you do on the test?"

"I don't know. We get the results back on Monday. I'll let you know then."

"What do you mean you don't know? You're the one who took the test!" Keisha replied, the pitch in her voice raising an octave.

"I mean, I knew some of the answers, but we're not even up to some of the questions he put on the test."

"Did you bring the textbook home?" Keisha asked.

"Yes, ma'am," he replied.

"Well, guess what? When you get up tomorrow morning, you will be studying instead of watching cartoons. And when you're done, I'm giving you a surprise quiz. Is that understood?"

"Yes, ma'am," Malik answered with a pitiful look on his face. "I've put all the groceries away. May I be excused?"

"Yes, you may, and thank you." Keisha said.

"Damn, Keisha, you go hard on them," Cece commented after Malik returned to his bedroom to finish playing his video game.

"That's how you got to handle these teenagers today, Cece. They'll walk all over you if you let them. You remember how we were."

"Yes, I do," Cece answered. "We were some sneaky little heifers."

"Yes, we were, and could lie our behinds off, too," Keisha said.

"Oh my God, Keisha, I just thought of something. Do you remember the sleepovers we used to have at my house?"

"Do I?" Keisha laughed at the thought. "We'd wait around for your mom to go to work, then get all made up and hit the clubs."

"And have our behinds back in the house before she did," Cece added.

"Yep, and still got up for Sunday school, hangover and all," Keisha said as the memories came back to her.

"Ooh, I used to hate that," said Cece.

"Did we ever get caught?" Keisha asked. "It was so long ago, I don't recall."

"Nope. We were too slick for them," Cece said. "But, I remember that one time when we almost did," she added.

"When?" asked Keisha.

"I think we were about sixteen at the time. We had our coats on and were about to walk out the door, when mama backtracked on us."

"Now I remember," Keisha recalled excitedly. "We jumped in the bed and got under the covers in a hurry when we heard that key turn in the door!"

"And we were still in our shoes!" Cece said, remembering like it was yesterday. "Those were the good old days. I sure do miss them."

"We did have some good times back then," Keisha agreed. "Were our parents that gullible? We got away with murder."

"I guess they were in a way. But, I think it was the amount of trust they put in us, more or less," Cece replied.

"And you see where that trust went, right?" Keisha asked.

"We were a mess," Cece admitted. "I now understand why you're so hard on the boys."

"Yeah, because I know how I used to be." Keisha stood up, walked to the fridge, and opened the door.

"You want a beer?"

"What kind you got?" Cece asked.

"What difference does it make? You gonna drink whatever I put in front of you, drunky," Keisha joked.

"Just give me the damn beer," Cece replied playfully.

Keisha returned to the table with two bottles of Busch and handed one to Cece, who looked at the beer oddly.

"What's this? Ain't you got a Bud or something? You can buy this cheap shit for $2.99 a case."

"Don't act like you don't want it," Keisha said.

"When have you ever known me to turn down a drink?" Cece said and cracked the lid off the bottle.

"Never, and that's why I bought it. I figured you'd be up here begging for something sooner or later," Keisha replied wittingly.

"Forget you, Keisha," Cece replied, raising the bottle to her lips. "Cheers," she said and took a long, big gulp.

"Cheers, drunky," replied Keisha, and they shared a laugh.

Cece took another sip of the beer before setting it down.

For a moment, there was silence, and neither of them spoke a word. Cece inattentively twirled her finger around the rim of the bottle, and her mind seemed to drift off into space. Keisha could sense something was wrong, because Cece always got quiet when something bothered her.

"What is it, Cece?"

"Come again?" she asked unknowingly.

"Don't even try it. I know you like a book. I can tell when my best friend is upset. You're too quiet."

Cece lifted her head from the table. Her eyes were filled with tears, and there was a look of sadness in them.

"Am I still your best friend, Keisha? Do you really feel that way?" she asked pitifully.

"Cece, we've been friends since I can remember. Why would you ask such a thing?" Keisha asked with concern.

"If we're such good friends, then why do you ignore me?"

"Where is this coming from, Cece? I don't understand." Keisha said, lighting a Newport. "When have I done that?"

"You do it all the time," Cece responded.

"How can you sit there and say that, Cece? Do I not stop and speak when we run into each other? Yes or no?"

"You know what I mean, Keisha. You'll stop for us to exchange a quick hello or goodbye, but that's it. I know you're ashamed of me, but it hurts when you do that," Cece confided.

Guilt overcame Keisha because some of the things Cece said were true. Keisha had kept silent during the early stages of Cece's drug dependency, when she first started using with Sonny. She sat on the sideline and watched as her best friend ruined her life, and she did nothing to stop it. It was a guilt that tormented Keisha for years. Since they were on the subject, Keisha decided to express her feelings. She held onto Cece's hand and spoke.

"I'm not ashamed of you, Cece. I'm ashamed of myself. I should have never let you get involved with Sonny and his influences. I should have intervened. I'm sorry, Cece. Can you ever forgive me?"

"Yeah, you should have done something, but I forgive you," Cece answered comically. Then she took one of the cigarettes from Keisha's pack. "And stop blaming yourself for my mistakes. Nobody made me do anything. I chose to do it."

"Cece, you need to get into a program that helps deal with substance abuse, and I'm going to see that you get through it this time," Keisha promised.

"Slow your role, Mother Teresa. It's already been done."

"For real?" Keisha asked excitedly.

"Yes. That's why I waited for you downstairs. I wanted to surprise you."

"I'm proud of you, girl. It took a lot of courage for you to take the first step. When do you start?"

"Next week, but I need a favor from you, Keisha."

"What is it, Cece?"

"Can you keep an eye on Jahlil for me while I'm away? You know, make sure he stays out of trouble."

"Don't I always?" Keisha remarked.

"I owe you one, girlfriend, and thanks for being honest with me."

"Don't worry about it, Cece. That's what friends are for," Keisha assured her. "Just make sure I have all of Jahlil's information before you leave. I'm getting him back into school come Monday morning, whether he likes it or not."

"That's been taken care of, too," Cece said. "I dragged his butt down to that school early this morning and got him enrolled."

"I don't believe it," Keisha said in a state of shock. "You've been on his behind about going to school for the longest. How did you get him to compromise?"

"It was easy," Cece replied. "I threatened to call the police and tell them he's selling pharmaceuticals if he didn't."

"And that worked?" Keisha asked.

"Girl, you should have seen how fast he moved when I picked up that phone and started dialing."

"I wish I could have been there to see that," Keisha said, laughing. "This calls for a celebration."

Keisha walked to the fridge and opened two Cokes. She gave one to Cece, and they raised the bottles.

"To the future, may it bring hope and prosperity," she said.

"Amen to that," Cece replied, and they clinked the bottles.

Author's Bio

Patron Gold was born in the inner city borough of Brooklyn, N.Y. He grew up in the Brownsville Housing Projects, until his family later relocated to Flatbush. In order to escape the social problems that surrounded his community, Gold developed a passion for reading at an early age. Music was also an interest that caught Gold's attention, and he embarked on a career as an R&B composer. He later realized he was able to express his creativity through his life's journey and travels, and crafted the novel *A House is a Broken Home*, which he successfully published in 2011.